# Hotel
# English
# 800

趙志敏 主編

# 飯店服務
# 英語800句

崧燁文化

# 目　　錄

# Preface 前言

　　我們根據飯店一線部門及單位工作的特點及飯店服務人員的現實情況，編寫了這本《飯店服務英語800句》，以滿足飯店服務人員工作及學習的需要。

　　本書由五大部分及附錄組成。五大部分即客務部、客房部、餐飲部、會展中心、康樂中心。附錄包括「飯店服務英語基本分類詞彙535個」、「中餐英文食譜」、「中式小吃」和「中外節日」。

　　本書內容條理清晰，簡潔實用，以英語單句為主，兼有少量對話，全部為中英對照。由於本書易學易用，它更是旅遊院校學生及飯店賓館工作人員提高自己飯店英語水平不可多得的自學教材。只要大家對照中文譯文，熟讀多記，靈活運用，一定能迅速提高自己的英語對客接待能力。

　　附錄裡的飯店服務英語基本分類詞彙分27　個類別，共計535個，是對飯店服務基本詞彙的彙總，如月份、星期、季節、部門、客房種類和客房用品及設備等，希望能對大家有所幫助。

　　在編寫過程中，我們努力使本書成為準確實用的資料工具書，但由於編者水平有限，書中若有疏漏不當之處，敬請廣大讀者和專家批評指正。

　　編者

# Part One Front Office Department 客務部

# Unit 1 Room Reservation 客房預訂

Ⅰ.Welcome

歡迎問候

1.Good morning (afternoon, evening), sir (ma'am).

早安（午安、晚安），先生（夫人）。

2.How do you do?

您好！（初次見面時）

3.Glad to meet you.

很高興見到您。

4.How are you?

您好嗎？

5.Fine, thanks. And you?

很好，謝謝。您也好吧？

6.Welcome to our hotel (restaurant, shop).

歡迎到我們飯店（餐廳、商店）來。

7.Wish you a most pleasant stay in our hotel.

願您在我們飯店過得愉快。

8.I hope you'll enjoy your stay with us.

希望您在我們飯店過得愉快。（客人剛入店時）

9.I hope you are enjoying your stay with us.

希望您在我們飯店過得愉快。（客人在飯店逗留期間）

10.I hope you have enjoyed your stay with us.

希望您在我們飯店過得愉快。（客人離店時）

11.Have a good time!

祝您過得愉快！

II.About Date

關於日期

12.When for?

您哪天要這個房間？

13.For what dates?

您要訂哪天的房？

14.Which date would that be?

那是哪一天？

15.Is it just for tonight?

只訂今天一個晚上嗎？

16.When do you need the room?

您什麼時候需要房間？

17.What time will you be here?

您什麼時間入住？

18.For how long?

您要住多久？

19.For how many nights?

您要住幾個晚上？

20.How long do you plan to stay?

您打算住多久？

21.How long will you be staying?

您要住多久？

Ⅲ.Receiving a Telephone Call

接電話

22.Hold on, please. I'll check it up for you.

請稍等，我查一下預訂情況。

23.Hold the line, please. I'll check the room availabilities for those dates.

請別掛電話，我查一下那幾天的預訂情況。

24.Thank you for waiting.

謝謝您耐心等待。

25.Sorry to have kept you waiting.

對不起，讓您久等了。

IV.About Room

關於房間

26.What kind of room would you like?

您想要什麼樣的房間？

27.Would you like a single or a double room?

您想要單人房還是雙人房？

28.We have deluxe suites, deluxe double rooms, twin-bed rooms with bath and single rooms. Which do you prefer?

我們這兒的房型有豪華套房、豪華雙人房、標準雙人房和單人房，您要哪一種？

29.Which do you prefer, a double room with bath or a

twinbed room with bath?

您是要帶浴室的雙人房還是要帶浴室的標準房？

30.Would you like a room with a front view or a rear view?

您是要臨街的還是背街的房間？

31.How many people will there be in your party?

你們一起有幾個人？

32.How many rooms would you like?

您想要幾個房間？

V.About Payment

關於付款方式

33.How will you be paying?

您將如何付款？

34.How would you like to make payment?

您打算以何種方式付款？

35.Who will be paying the bill?

誰將支付費用？

36.Is the company willing to cover all the expenses?

公司是否願意支付所有費用？

37.Which company do you work for?

您為哪個公司工作？

38.You'll have to send us a deposit of 100 USD.

您需要寄給我們100美元的押金。

## VI.About Cost

關於費用

39.For a single room the price would be 200 USD.

單人房的價格是200美元。

40.A double room costs 250 USD.

一間雙人房價格是250美元。

41.Breakfast is also included.

早餐也包括在內。

42.The total cost would be 480 USD.

全部費用是480美元。

43.The rate includes three full meals.

此價格包括三頓正餐。

44.We'll give you 10 percent off.

我們可以給您打九折。

45.I can give you 15 percent discount.

我可以給您15%的折扣。

## VII.About Arrival Date and Time

關於抵達日期和時間

46.What time will you be arriving?

您將何時到達？

47.Will you be arriving before 8 a.m.?

您是在上午8點前到達嗎？

48.Will you be arriving after 4 p.m?

您是在下午4點之後到達嗎？

49.Will you be coming by plane?

您將乘飛機來嗎？

50.Could you give me your flight number, please, in case the plane is late？

請問您的航班號是多少，以防出現飛機誤點的情況？

51.Could I have the flight number and arrival time?

請將您的航班號和到達時間告訴我，好嗎？

VIII.About Guests' Name and Address

關於客人姓名和聯繫地址

52.Could you give me your name, please?

請問您貴姓？

53.May I have your name and initials, please?

請問您的姓名和名字的首寫字母是什麼？

54.Who's the reservation for?

您為誰預訂房間？

55.What's your address, please?

請告訴我您的地址，好嗎？

IX.Confirming a Reservation

預訂確認

56.Your reservelation is confirmed.

您的預訂被確認了。

57.You can have the room then.

屆時您可以入住預訂的房間。

58.We have single rooms available on those dates.

那幾天我們有空閒的單人房。

59.I can book you a double room for the 16thand 17th.

我可以為您在16、17日訂一個雙人房。

Ⅹ.The Reservation Is Not Confirmed

預訂沒有被確認

60.We don't have any single rooms available.Would you mind a double room instead?

我們沒有單人房了，雙人房行嗎？

61.I cannot let you have one on the fourth floor.

我無法在四樓為您安排一間房。

62.Unfortunately, we're fully booked for the 25th, but we can guarantee you a room for the 26th.

很遺憾，25 號那天房間全部訂滿，但26 號我可以保證為您留一間房。

63.I'm sorry, I can't book you a room for the 7th and 8th.

對不起，我無法為您訂7號和8號的房間。

64.We're booked solid for all kinds of rooms on that night.

那天所有的客房全部訂滿。

65.If there isn't any room, we can get you on a waiting list or we can find you a room in another hotel.

如沒有空房間，我們可以記下您的名字，一旦有空房間就給您安排，或者為您在其他飯店找個房間。

66.This is the busiest season. I'm very sorry, but could you call us again later this week? We may have a cancellation.

現在是旅遊旺季，很抱歉，請您在這週後幾天再打電話過來好嗎？也許會有人取消預訂。

67.Is it possible for you to change your reservation date? We do have rooms available on the following day.

您可以改變您的預訂日期嗎？我們第二天就有空房了。

XI.About the Hotel

關於飯店情況

68.Our hotel is a 4-star hotel with good reputation.

我們是一家信譽良好的四星級飯店。

69.Our hotel is beautifully situated.

我們飯店環境優美。

70.Our hotel is located in the center of the city.

我們飯店位於市中心。

71.Our hotel is close to the business district.

我們飯店靠近商業區。

72.Our hotel is near the downtown area.

我們飯店靠近市區繁華地帶。

73.It takes only 15 minutes' drive from our hotel to the airport.

從我們飯店開車去機場只需15分鐘。

74.Our hotel is conveniently situated, only minutes from banks, shopping centers and major attractions.

我們飯店地理位置優越，靠近銀行、商場和主要景點。

75.Our hotel is very modern and comfortable.

我們飯店服務設施先進，環境舒適。

76.There are 500 rooms in our hotel.

我們飯店有500間客房。

77.We offer baby-sitting service.

我們提供保姆服務。

78.No guests are allowed to bring pets or animals into the hotel.

客人不得攜帶寵物或其他動物進入飯店。

79.Our hotel faces the sea.

我們飯店面朝大海。

80.You can have a bird's-eye view of the city on the top of our hotel.

在我們飯店頂樓您可以鳥瞰整個城市。

81.You can overlook a beautiful park in your room.

在房間您就可以看到一個美麗的公園。

XII.Looking Forward to Guests' Arrival

期待客人的到來

82.We look forward to seeing you.

我們恭候您的光臨。

83.We'll be expecting you next Monday.

我們下星期一見。

# Unit 2 Check-in 登記入住

Ⅰ.Receiving Guests with a Reservation

有預訂客人登記入住

84.Welcome to our hotel.

歡迎下榻我們飯店。

85.Do you have a reservation with us?

您有預訂嗎？

86.That was a single room，wasn't it?

您預訂的是一間單人房，對嗎？

87.Will you register，please?

請您登記。

88.Would you register individually · please?

請你們分開登記，好嗎？

89.Will you complete the registration form · please?

請您填寫登記表。

90.Please fill in the registration form.

請填寫登記表。

91.Could you please put your nationality here?

請將您的國籍寫在這兒。

92.Could I ask you to put your name in block capitals?

請用大寫字母書寫您的名字.

93.What's your occupation, please ?

請問您的職業？

94.What's your address in your native country, please?

請問您在貴國的地址是什麼？

95.Sign here, please.

請在這兒簽名。

96.Could you sign your name, please?

請您簽名。

97.May I see your passport?

可以看看您的護照嗎？

98.Your passport, please.

請出示護照。

99.Have you got any identification?

您有什麼可以證明您身份的證件嗎？

100.Show me your ID card, please.

請出示您的身份證件。

101.We have a room reserved for you.

我們有您預訂的房間。

102.Here's your room card.

這是您的房卡。

103.Here's your room key.

這是您的房間鑰匙。

104.Could you keep your room key until you check out?

請您在住店期間自己保管鑰匙，直到離店。

105.Your room number is 1508, on the 15th floor.

您的房間是1508，在十五層。

106.A bellboy will show you to your room.

行李員會帶您去您的房間。

107.Please take Mr.White's suitcase up to Room 1508, will
you？

請幫懷特先生拿行李，帶他到1508房間。

108.The elevator is over there, on your right.

電梯在那兒，您的右手邊。

109.Enjoy your stay with us.

希望您在我們這兒住得愉快。

110.Have a nice day!

祝您愉快！

II.Check-in Dispute

入住糾紛

111.What name was it, please?

請問您以什麼名字預訂的房間？

112.In whose name was the reservation made?

請問房間預訂在誰的名下？

113.Who made the reservation, please?

請問誰做的預訂？

114.When did you make the reservation?

請問您什麼時候訂的房？

115.When was it made?

什麼時候訂的？

116.What was the date of the reservation?

請問您預訂房間的日期。

117.From which country?

從哪個國家？

118.Do you remember the name of the reservation clerk?

您還記得接待您的人員名字嗎？

119.Can you spell that for me, please?

請您拼寫一下，好嗎？

120.How do you spell your name, please?

請問怎麼拼寫您的名字？

121.I'm sorry, but I haven't got any record of that.

對不起，我們這裡沒有您預訂的記錄。

122.I'm sorry, but there is no record of that.

對不起，我們沒有您預訂的記錄。

123.I'm sorry, we have no record of a reservation in your name.

對不起，沒有以您的名字預訂的記錄。

124.Do you have a fax confirming the reservation?

您收到過確認預訂的傳真嗎？

125.The room may have been reserved in the name of the person who made the reservation.

房間可能預訂在為您做預訂的那人的名下了。

Ⅲ.When the Room Is Not Ready

房間還沒準備好

126.I'm afraid your room is not ready yet. Would you mind waiting a moment, please? We are very sorry for the inconvenience.

恐怕您的房間還沒收拾好，請您稍等一會兒，好嗎？給您帶來不便，真對不起。

## IV.Changing Rooms or Extending a Reservation

換房間或者延長預訂時間

127.We'll extend the reservation for you.

我們可以為您延長預訂時間。

128.We'll make the change for you.

我們可以給您換個房間。

129.You may keep the room till 3 p.m., if you like.

如果您願意，可以將房間保留到下午三點。

130.By how many nights do you wish to extend?

您希望延長幾個晚上？

131.If we weren't so heavily booked, we would let you stay in the room till 4 p.m. free of charge.

如果不是因為我們房間緊張，我們可以免費讓您在房間呆到下午4點。

132.We've got a full house, so if you really want to keep your room this afternoon, we'll have to charge you 50% of the price.

我們客房很緊，如果您確實需要再住一個下午，恐怕我們要向您收50%的房費。

133.The hotel is full and there'll be someone taking your room. We'll keep your luggage if you like.

我們飯店現已客滿，您的房間有人要住進去。如果您願意，我們可以為您保管行李。

134.I'm afraid you'll have to vacate your room by 11. I must apologize for the inconvenience.

非常抱歉，恐怕您得在11點以前搬出房間。給您帶來不便，我深表歉意。

135.Your room has been booked for tomorrow. Would you mind changing rooms?

您的房間明晚已預訂給別人了。請您換個房間，好嗎？

# Unit 3 Bellboy Service 行李生服務

136.The reception desk is just over there. This way, please.

櫃臺就在那兒，這邊請。

137.Let me help you with your baggage.

我來幫您拿行李。

138.How many pieces of baggage do you have in all?

您一共有幾件行李？

139.I'll show you up to your room.

我來領您去房間。

140.Is this your first time to stay in our hotel?

您是第一次住我們飯店嗎？

141.May I have a look at your room card?

讓我看一下您的房卡，好嗎？

142.Here we are.

我們到了。

143.After you, sir.

先生，你先請。

144.Here is Room 1508. May I have your key?

1508房到了，請您把鑰匙給我。

145.I'm sure you'll like your room.

您肯定會喜歡您的房間的。

146.If you need anything, just call the reception. The number is 0.

如有什麼需要，請撥0與櫃臺聯繫。

147.The bathroom is here on the left. And here's the closet.

左邊是盥洗室，這兒是壁櫥。

148.If you need anything, please refer to the hotel services directory.

如需要什麼，請參閱飯店服務指南。

149.Please leave your laundry in the laundry bag.

請將要洗的衣服放在洗衣袋裡。

150.Do you need a wake-up call in the morning?

早晨需要叫您起床嗎？

151.The coffee shop is open 24 hours.

咖啡廳24小時營業。

152.Here's our hotel card. You can show it to the taxi driver.

這是我們飯店的名片。您可以把它向計程車司機出示。

153.There is a souvenir shop on the second floor.

二樓有一間紀念品店。

154.You can either take a taxi or take bus No.1 to go there.

您可以乘計程車或乘1路公共汽車去那裡。

155.There are many scenic spots in our city.

我們這座城市有很多風景點。

156.I'll call a taxi for you.

我幫您叫部計程車。

# Unit 4 Information Desk 詢問處

157.Can I take a message for you?

您要留言嗎？

158.Would you like to leave a message?

您想留言嗎？

159.I'm sorry, he is out. He won't be back until six.

對不起，他出去了，得到六點鐘才回來。

160.I'm afraid we don't know at what time he left the hotel.

抱歉，我們不知道他什麼時間離開飯店的。

161.I'm afraid he has already checked out.

對不起，他已經結帳退房了。

162.I'm sorry, he left yesterday.

對不起，他昨天就退房了。

163.I'm sorry, he left for Taipei this morning.

對不起，他今天早晨剛剛離開去台北了。

164.I'm afraid he has cancelled his reservation.

抱歉，他取消了預訂。

165.I'm sorry, there's no such a person he re.Is he a hotel guest ?

對不起，沒有這個人，他住我們飯店嗎？

166.I'm sorry, I can't find his name on the register list.

對不起，我在客人登記表上找不到他的名字。

167.I'm afraid he isn't staying in our hotel.

恐怕他沒住我們飯店。

168.I'm afraid there is no guest with that name. But we have a guest with a similar name. Would that be him ?

抱歉，這裡沒有客人叫這個名字，但我們有位客人的名字和這

個名字相似，會不會是他？

169.I'm afraid he is out for the day. Could you call again later, please?

恐怕他整個白天都不在，您能不能晚些時候再打電話過來？

170.Would you leave a message? We'll inform him when he comes back.

您要不要留言？等他回來時我們可以轉告他。

171.I'm afraid we can only take simple messages.

抱歉，我們只能轉達簡短的口信。

172.What's your telephone number in case he wants to call you?

請問您的電話號碼是多少？也許他想給您打電話。

173.What's your phone number in case he has forgotten?

請問您的電話號碼，萬一他忘了您的號碼？

174.I'll repeat your message.

我來重複一下您的留言。

175.Is that the message?

這就是您的留言嗎？

176.There is a message for you from Mr.James Brown. He called at 4：40 p.m. and asked you to call him back as soon as you returned.His number is 6595-1122.

這是詹姆斯·布朗先生給您的留言，他下午4：40打電話來讓您一回來就給回電話，他的號碼是6595-1122。

177.Mr.Green is here for his appointment.

格林先生來赴約了。

178.There is a gentleman by the name of Smith who wants to see you.

有一位叫史密斯的先生要求見您。

179.There is a Mr.Black who wants to see you. Shall I ask him to go up?

有一位布萊克先生要求見您，我請他上去嗎？

180.He is meeting somebody. He can't see you right now.

他在會見客人，現在不能見您。

181.I'm afraid you can't see her right now. She is at the hairdresser's.

恐怕這會兒您不能馬上見到她，她在美容院呢。

182.He asked us to tell you to meet him in the coffee shop.

他讓轉告您，他將在咖啡廳和您見面。

# Unit 5 Switchboard Operator 總機服務

183.Who is speaking, please?

請問您是哪位？

184.May I ask who is calling, please?

請問是哪位？

185.This is Mr.Li speaking.

我是李先生。

186.Mr.Clark speaking.Who is calling, please?

我是克拉克先生，請問您是哪位？

187.May I speak to Mr.Brown, please?

請問布朗先生在嗎？

188.There are two Mr.Browns in the hotel. Could you please give me his first name?

我們飯店有兩位姓布朗的先生，您能告訴我您要找的那位先生的名字嗎？

189.Would you put me through to the Front Desk?

請幫我轉客務部。

190.I beg your pardon?

請再說一遍。

191.Hold on, please.

請稍等。

192.Please hold the line while I try to connect you.

請別掛線，我來給您接通。

193.Mr.Wang, you're through.Mr.Li's number is ringing.

王先生，電話接通了。李先生的電話響了。

194.Could you hold on a minute? I'll get him for you.

請稍等，我去找他來。

195.Mr.Brown, phone call for you.

布朗先生，您的電話。

196.Mr.Brown, you're wanted on the phone.

布朗先生，有您的電話。

197.Sorry, the line is busy.

對不起，電話占線。

198.The line is engaged.

占線。

199.The line is dead.

電話掉線了。

200.The line has been cut off.

電話中斷了。

201.The line has been disconnected.

電話中斷了。

202.I've been connected to the wrong party. Could you reconnect me, please?

剛才搞錯了，重新幫我接一下，好嗎？

203.There is a call for you.Shall I put him/her through?

有電話找您，用我幫您接過來嗎？

204.He's on another line now.

他在接打另一個電話。

205.He's not in at the moment. Would you like to leave a message?

他這會兒不在，您要留言嗎？

206.He's out. Would you like to speak to someone else?

他出去了，別人接，行嗎？

207.He's out on business today.

他今天因公外出了。

208.Would you call him later?

您過會再打給他，好嗎？

209.He's occupied at the moment. Would you mind waiting?

他這會兒正忙著呢。您稍等一會兒，好嗎？

210.He's not available now.

他這會兒正忙著呢（或，他這會兒不在）。

211.There's no one by the name of Liu Ming here. Would you check it?

我們這裡沒有叫劉明的，請您再核對一下。

212.I'm afraid you've dialed the wrong number.

恐怕您打錯了。

213.Sorry, wrong number.

對不起，打錯了。

214.Please consult the telephone directory.

請查電話簿。

215.I'd like to place a wake-up call.

我想預訂叫醒服務。

216.At what time, please？

請問幾點鐘？

217.At what time shall we call you?

我們幾點叫醒您？

218.At what time would you like us to call you?

您希望我們幾點鐘叫醒您？

219.You may use the computer automatic wake-up system.

您可以使用電腦自動叫醒服務系統。

220.Please dial 5 first, then the time you want. Say 6: 30, you dial 0630. Be sure there are 5 digits in the final number.

請先撥5，然後是時間。比如說6：30，您就撥0630。請確定最後顯示的必須有五位數。

221.The computer will record your room number and the time automatically.

電腦會自動記錄您的房間號和時間。

222.If someone calls me, will you connect him or her with my voice mail, please?

如果有人打電話找我，能否幫我接通語音留言？

223.Sorry, I can't tell you the guest's extension number.

對不起，我不能告訴您客人的房間電話號碼。

224.The guest's extension number is confidential.

我們客人的房間電話號碼不對外公開。

225.Thanks for calling.

謝謝垂詢。

226.Thank you for your calling.

謝謝您打來電話。

# Unit 6 Foreign Currency Exchange
## 外幣兌換

227.Would you like to change some money?

您要換匯嗎？

228.How would you like to change?

您想怎麼換？

229.I want to change some US dollars into TWD

我想把一些美元換成台幣。

230.How much would you like to change?

您要換多少？

231.We change foreign currencies according to today's exchange rate.

我們根據今天的外匯牌價來兌換外幣。

232.Our buying rate for notes is 3000 NTD for 100 US dollars.

今天的現金買入牌價是3000元台幣兌100美元。

233.Our buying rate for notes is 3500 NTD for 100 Euros.

今天的現金買入價是3500元台幣兌100歐元。

234.100 Euros, an equivalent of 3500 NTD.

100歐元可兌換台幣3500元。

235.Please fill in the exchange memo, your passport number and the total sum, and then sign your name.

請在水單上填寫您的護照號碼和兌換金額，然後簽名。

237.What denomination do you need?

請問您需要什麼樣面值的？

238.There are 1000-NTD notes, 500-NTD notes, 100-NTD notes, and coins.

有1000元、500元、100 元的紙幣，還有硬幣。

239.Give me one 1000-NTD notes, one 500-NTD notes, one 100-NTD  notes and the others are 1-NTD coins.

給我1張1000 元的，1 張500 元的紙幣，1 張100 元的紙幣，其他都要1元的硬幣。

240.Here's 1642 NTD. Please Check it and keep the memo.

這是您的1642元，請點一下，並請保存好水單。

# Unit 7 Ticket Booking 訂票服務

241.I'd like to book a plane ticket.

我想訂張機票。

242.Where are you flying to?

您要飛往哪裡？

243.I'd like to book a seat on a flight from Teipei to Shanghai on the 2nd of October, please.

我想訂個10月2日台北飛往上海的機位。

244.Which airline are you planning to take?

您打算乘坐什麼航班？

245.When are you leaving?

您什麼時候走？

246.Do you want a morning or an afternoon flight?

您想要上午的還是下午的航班？

247.There is a flight leaving at 16: 30 in the afternoon. Will that be okay with you?

下午16：30有一個航班，您覺得可以嗎？

248.I'm afraid that flight is fully booked.

恐怕那個航班已訂滿了。

249.There are seats available on a flight leaving at 17: 30.

17：30起飛的航班還有機位。

250.May I have your name and room number, please?

請問您姓名和房間號碼？

251.May I see your passport and room card, please?

讓我看看您的護照和房卡，好嗎？

252.First-class or economy?

您要頭等艙還是經濟艙？

253.Single or return fare?

單程還是往返票？

254.Please sign your name here.

請在這兒簽名。

255.How many tickets do you need?

您需要幾張票？

256.There are not any 10000-NTD ones left.

10000元的已經沒有了。

257.We'd like to sit together.

我們想坐在一起。

258.We charge 5000 NTD in advance. Come to fetch the tickets this evening.

請預付5000元。今天晚上來取票。

# Unit 8 Asking and Directing the Way 問路指路

259.—Can you tell me the way to the coffee shop, please?

請問去咖啡廳怎麼走？

—The bellman will show you the way.

服務生會為您指路的。

260.—Excuse me, where is the Chinese restaurant?

請問，中餐廳在哪兒？

—I'll show you the way myself.

我來領你們去。

261.—We're looking for the bank.

我們要找銀行。

—It's just over there，behind you.

就在您身後那邊。

262.—Could you direct us to the coffee shop?

你能告訴我們去咖啡廳怎麼走嗎？

—Go straight through the cafeteria, and you'll find it just in front of you.

一直往前走，穿過自助餐廳，對面就是咖啡廳。

263.—I wonder if you could tell me where the health club

is.

你能否告訴我健身房在哪兒？

—It's round here to the left. Follow the sign marked sauna and it's just next door to that.

從這兒向左拐，順著桑拿的標誌走，健身房就在桑拿室隔壁。

264.—Which way is the phone booth, please?

請問去電話廳怎麼走？

—Along there to your left. It's just past the ladies'room, opposite the elevator.

向左走，過了女洗手間，電梯對面就是。

265.—Is this the right way for the souvenir shop?

去禮品店，是從這兒走嗎？

—Yes.Along the corridor，past the newsstand.

是的，順著樓道往前走，過了報攤就是。

266.—Is the lobby bar somewhere hereabouts?

大堂酒吧就在附近嗎？

—It's right behind you, sir, but I'm afraid it's not open till 11.

就在您身後，先生，但是恐怕11點才開始營業。

267.—Am I going the right way for the tennis courts?

去網球場是這條路嗎？

—Along the corridor to your right, then turn left. Go

down the stairs, along a bit further and out into the yard.

順著您右手樓梯走，然後左拐，下樓梯，再往前走幾步，出門進了院子就是。

268.—I'm looking for the conference No.4.

我要找四號會議室。

—They're all facing the open lounge. Walk along to your right, past the elevators and up the stairs.

會議室都在公共休息室對面，順著右邊走，過電梯上樓就是。

# Unit 9 Checkout 結帳離店

269.Are you checking out today?

您今天要退房嗎？

270.What's your room number, please?

請問您的房間號是多少？

271.Were you in Room 1201?

您是住1201房嗎？

272.Are you Mr.Brown?

您是布朗先生嗎？

273.May I have your name and room number?

請告訴我您的姓名和房號。

274.Did you make any phone calls from your room?

您從您房間打過電話嗎？

275.How many phone calls did you make?

您打過幾個電話？

276.Did you take anything from the minibar this morning?

您今天早上是否從客房小冰箱裡取過東西？

277.Let me figure it out.

我把您的帳算出來。

278.That comes to 320.

總共是320美元。

279.That'll be 2100 Yuan.

共計2100元。

280.Here's your bill.Please check it.

這是您的帳單，請您過目。

281.Would you like to check it?

請您核對一下，好嗎？

282.Would you like to check and see if there's any mistakes?

請您核對一下，看是否有誤？

283.This is for the phone calls you made from your room.

這是您從房間打電話的費用。

284.That's for the laundry.

那是洗衣費。

285.The service charge is included in the bill.

這個帳單包括服務費。

286.How would you like to pay, in cash, with checks or by credit cards?

請問您想以何種方式付帳，現金、支票還是信用卡？

287.What's your way of payment, please?

您想怎麼付帳？

288.What kind have you got?

您用的是哪一種？

289.What credit card do you have?

您的是哪種信用卡？

290.Sorry, we don't accept personal checks.

對不起，我們不收私人支票。

291.It's the policy of the hotel.

這是店規。

292.You'll have to give me your name and address.

請告訴我您的姓名和地址。

293.Please show me your passport or some other identification.

請出示您的護照或者其他證件。

294.May I have the card, please?

請把卡給我。

295.May I have a print of your card?

我可以把您的卡複印一份嗎？

296.Since the amount exceeds 12000 NTD, we have to get the approval code.

由於總額超過12000元台幣，我們必須得知道授權號碼才行。

297.Here's your receipt.

這是您的收據。

298.Thank you. I hope you've enjoyed your stay here.

謝謝，希望您在本店住得愉快。

299.How do you like our hotel?

您覺得我們飯店怎麼樣？

300.It's very kind of you to say so.

謝謝您這麼說。

301.Hope you will come and stay with us again.

希望您再次光臨我們飯店。

302.Have a good flight.

祝您旅途愉快。

303.Have a pleasant journey home.

祝您歸途愉快。

# Part Two Housekeeping Department 客房部

## Unit 10 Chamber Service 客房服務

1.The electric current in your room is 220 volts.

您房間的電壓是220伏。

2.The minibar will be replenished on a daily basis.

小冰箱的食品和飲料每天補充一次。

3.If you need anything, please don't hesitate to call.

如有任何需要，請隨時打電話。

4.Ice cubes are in your minibar or dial 6 for room service.

小冰箱裡有冰塊，您也可以撥 6，送餐中心將會送冰塊來。

5.I'll turn on/off the air-conditioning/heat.

我給您打開/關上空調/暖氣。

6.I'll turn up/down the air-conditioning/heat.

我給您調高/調低空調/暖氣。

7.I'll bring in some fresh towels.

我去拿乾淨毛巾。

8.I'd like one more blanket.I feel a little bit cold.

我想再要一床毛毯，我覺得有點冷。

9.I'll have it sent to your room immediately.

我馬上叫人給您送過來。

10.I'll send someone up with it right away.

我馬上派人給您送上來。

11.When do you need it ?

您什麼時候需要？

12.May I have some more writing-paper?

再給我一些信紙，好嗎？

13.Did you sleep well last night ?

昨晚睡得好嗎？

14.I have a cold.

我感冒了。

15.I have a bad headache/stomachache.

我頭／肚子痛得厲害。

16.Do you have a temperature?

您發燒嗎？

17.Would you like to see a doctor?

需要看醫生嗎？

18.You'd better go to see a doctor.

您最好去看一下醫生。

19.Please take a good rest and I hope you'll get well soon.

希望您好好休息，早日恢復健康。

20.Do you feel better now?

您現在感覺好點了嗎？

# Unit 11 Room Cleaning 客房清掃

21.May I come in?

我可以進來嗎？

22.Sorry to disturb you, but may I clean your room now?

對不起打擾一下，現在可以打掃您的房間嗎？

23.May I make the beds now?

請問現在可以為您鋪床嗎？

24.May I do the turn-down service now?

現在幫您整理房間，好嗎？

25.Will you come back later?

請你過會兒再來，好嗎？

26.What time would be convenient, sir?

先生，請問幾點鐘比較方便？

27.Would it be convenient if I return at 9: 30?

我九點半再來，方便嗎？

28.I'll come and clean your room immediately.

我馬上來打掃您的房間。

29.Can I make the beds for you now or later?

請問是現在還是再過一會兒為您鋪床？

30.When would you like those done for?

您希望什麼時候把這些給您做了？

31.I have a section of 14 rooms and I always do the check-out rooms first unless there is a request.

我要打掃14間客房，如無客人要求先打掃，我總是先打掃走客房。

32.May I refill your minibar?

我來補充冰箱裡的食品飲料。

# Unit 12 Laundry Service 洗衣服務

33.Do you have any laundry, sir?

先生，有要洗的衣服嗎？

34.If you have some laundry, please leave it in the laundry bag.

如需洗衣，請把衣服放在洗衣袋裡。

35.You'll find a laundry bag and list in your closet.

洗衣袋和洗衣單在壁櫥裡。

36.Please fill in the laundry list.

請填寫洗衣單。

37.Please refer to your laundry list for further information.

洗衣單上有詳細說明，請查閱。

38.Please don't forget to fill out the laundry form; otherwise our list must be accepted as correct.

請別忘了填寫洗衣單，否則一律以我們統計的洗衣單為準。

39.Would you like express service?

您需要快洗服務嗎？

40.We have express service.

我們有快洗服務。

41.We also provide express service, but it will cost 50% more.

我們提供快洗服務，但加收50%費用。

42.Express service charge is double the regular service.

快洗服務加倍收費。

43.Express service takes only 3 hours.

快洗服務只需3個小時。

44.The laundry account will be charged on your master account.

洗衣費將匯入您的總帳單。

45.Laundry fee will be added to your bill or you can pay it when they are back.

洗衣費將匯入您的帳單，您也可以在收到洗好的衣物時付帳。

46.When can I have them back?

什麼時候可以洗好取回？

47.When will it be ready?

什麼時候能洗好？

48.We collect the laundry at 9: 00 every morning and return it to you by 4: 00 p.m.the same day.

收衣時間是每天早上 9 點鐘，當天下午 4 點鐘送衣進房。

49.Laundry will be collected at about 9: 00 every day.

每天早上9點收要洗的衣服。

50.They will be back to you at 4 p.m.

下午4點就給您送回來。

51.I'd like to have my overcoat dry-cleaned, my shirt and pajamas laundered and my suit pressed.

我的大衣要乾洗，襯衫和睡衣要水洗，西裝需要熨一下。

52.I don't want the shirt starched.

這件襯衣不要上漿。

53.Is your dress colorfast?

您的衣服不褪色吧？

54.Will the color run?

會掉色嗎？

55.Don't worry. We'll dry-clean the dress.The color won't run.

別擔心，我們乾洗這件衣服，就不會褪色了。

56.A button is missing on your blouse.

您上衣的一粒紐扣掉了。

57.We can mend it.

我們可以織補。

58.We can mend a seam, not a hole.

我們可以補一條縫，不能補一個洞。

59.Your coat has been mended. Is it all right?

您的大衣補好了，您看可以嗎？

60.We'll do our best to remove the stain.

我們會盡力去除這個汙點。

61.You'll find your laundry in your closet.

您的衣服洗好後會放在壁櫥裡。

62.Here's your laundry.

這是為您洗好的衣服。

63.—May I have the misdelivered items?

請把送錯的衣服給我。

—Sorry for the inconvenience.

對不起，給您帶來了不便。

64.There is no need to compensate.

不用賠償了。

# Unit 13 Lost and Found 失物招領

65.What's the matter?

怎麼了？

66.Sorry to hear that.

聽到這事，我感到很遺憾。

67.When and where did you last see it?

您最後一次見到它是什麼時候，在什麼地方？

68.When and where did you first miss it?

您最早發現丟失東西是什麼時候，在什麼地方？

69.Where did you leave it?

您把它放哪兒了？

70.We have checked our lost and found list, but I'm afraid your camera didn't appear on it.

我們查了一下失物招領單，很遺憾沒有發現您的相機。

71.Could you fill out this form with your address and the value and description of the camera?

請您填一下這個表，寫上您的地址及照相機的價值和情況說明，好嗎？

72.Could you fill out the lost property form, please?

請填寫一下失物登記表，好嗎？

73.If we locate it, we'll send it to you by airmail.

如果找到了，我們會用航空郵件寄給您的。

74.We'll contact you if it is located.

如果找到了，我們會跟您聯繫。

75.What make is it?

什麼牌子的？

76.What brand is it?

什麼牌子？

77.What color is it?

什麼顏色？

78.What size is it?

多大尺寸？

79.What style is it?

什麼樣式？

80.What is the value of your camera?

您的相機價值多少錢？

81.What is it made of?

是什麼材質的？

82.How many items are there?

有幾樣東西？

83.What is in it?

裡面有什麼？

84.Was it a man's or a lady's watch?

是男式表還是女式表？

# Unit 14 Damage and Maintenance 損壞與維修

85.I'm the housekeeper. May I know what happened here?

我是客房部主管，請問這兒發生什麼事了？

86.I'm sorry to hear that. Let me take a look first.

真糟糕，讓我先看一下。

87.I'm sorry to say they are badly damaged.

對不起，但我不得不說它們被損壞得很嚴重。

88.I'm afraid we have to charge them to your account.

恐怕我們必須向您收取賠償金。

89.I'll ask the chambermaid to bring a new bedcover and a blanket for this evening.

我讓客房服務員給您拿一條新床單和一條毛毯來。

90.What's the matter?

出什麼問題了？

91.Is there anything to be repaired ?

有什麼要修的嗎？

92.The television isn't working.

電視機壞了。

93.The toilet is stopped up.

馬桶堵了。

94.The toilet is blocked.

馬桶堵塞了。

95.The toilet is overflowing.

馬桶往外溢水了。

96.There is no water in the toilet.

馬桶裡無水。

97.The flush isn't working.

馬桶不能沖水了。

98.There is something wrong with the showerhead (sink, toilet, tap, desk-lamp)

淋浴噴頭（洗手池、馬桶、水龍頭、臺燈）壞了。

99.The desk-lamp is broken/out of order.

臺燈壞了。

100.The heating is off.

暖氣停了。

101.The power is off.

停電了。

102.The sink is leaking/clogged.

洗手池漏水 / 堵了。

103.The water tap drips all night.

水龍頭滴了一整夜水。

104.The light bulb has blown.

燈泡燒了。

105.I will check into it.

我會調查一下此事。

106.I'll take care of it personally.

我會親自去解決這件事的。

107.A repairman/electrician will come and check it right away.

修理工 / 電工馬上就會來檢查一下。

108.I'll send for the plumber.

我去叫水管工來。

109.I'm sorry for that. I'll tell the manager of the Maintenance Department.He'll deal with it at once.

我對此表示歉意，我會通知維修部的經理，他會立即處理此事。

110.We'll send someone up to repair it.

我們會派人去修的。

111.We're very sorry for the inconvenience.The night manager will come immediately.

很抱歉給您帶來了不便，夜班經理馬上就來。

112.Maintenance can be in your room in 15 minutes.

維修工15分鐘後就到您房間。

113.We're trying to find the cause. Could you wait a little longer, please ?

我們正在查找原因，請您再等一會兒，好嗎？

114.We'll bring a replacement immediately.

我們馬上給您換一個。

115.I'll fix it for you.

我來為您修理。

116.Please wait just a few minuses. It won't be long.

請等一會兒，很快就好。

117.We can have it repaired.

我們可以修好它。

118.We'll have it repaired at once.

我們馬上開始修理。

119.Some parts need to be replaced. I'll be back soon.

要換幾個零件，我去取，很快就回來。

120.Do you mind if I remove your things？

可以將您的東西挪一下嗎？

121.It's all right now. You may try it.

修好了，您可以試一下。

122.I'm sorry, but we can't fix it today.

很抱歉，今天修不好了。

123.We do wish we had known it earlier.

要是早點知道這個情況就好了。

124.I guarantee that this won't happen again.

我保證此事不會再發生。

125.Since the water pipes are being repaired, cold water is not available from 8 a.m to 3 p.m.

由於正在修水管，從上午8點到下午3點，暫停供水。

126.We do apologize for the inconvenience.

給您帶來了不便，我們深表歉意。

127.We appreciate your cooperation.

多謝您的合作。

128.Thank you for your understanding.

謝謝您的理解。

129.Thanks for your cooperation.

謝謝合作。

# Part Three Food & Beverage Department 餐飲部

# Unit 15 Food&Beverage Reservation
## 餐飲預訂

1.I'd like to book a table for four for this evening at 7: 30.

我想訂一張今晚7: 30的四人桌。

2.What time do you open this evening?

你們今晚幾點鐘開始營業？

3.We open at 6: 00 p.m.and close at midnight.

我們從晚上6點至午夜營業。

4.I'm sorry, we're not open at 5: 30 p.m.

對不起，我們下午5：30還沒開始營業。

5.We're open until midnight.

我們營業至午夜。

6.We open 24 hours.

我們24小時營業。

7.We open round the clock.

我們不分晝夜都營業。

8.I'm sorry. we're not open on Mondays.

對不起，我們星期一不營業。

9.When would that be for?

請問訂哪一天的餐位？

10.For what time?

您要訂什麼時間的？

11.For how many?

一共有幾位？

12.How many people are there in your party?

你們一共有幾位？

13.How many would that be for?

一共有幾位？

14.Who's the reservation for?

請問訂在誰的名下？

15.May I have your name?

請問您貴姓？

16.What time will you be arriving?

請問您幾點鐘到？

17.How much per head would you like to spend?

請問您訂什麼標準的？ / 您打算每位花多少錢？

18.What rate do you have in mind?

您想按什麼樣的標準用餐？

19.What is it going to be, Chinese food or Western food?

您要中餐還是西餐？

20.Would you like a table in the main restaurant or in a VIP room?

您要大廳餐位還是包廂？

21.Would you like to sit by the window or near the doorway?

您想坐靠窗坐還是靠門口？

22.Anything special you'd like to have on the menu?

您對菜單有什麼特別要求嗎？

23.Do you have any special wishes as regards the food?

您對食物有什麼特別要求嗎？

24.At what time have you planned to hold the banquet?

宴會定在幾點鐘開始？

25.Do you have our banqueting information pack?

您有我們的宴會訊息介紹單嗎？

26.What sort of table plan do you have in mind?

您希望餐桌擺成何種形式？

27.What type of service would you require?

您需要何種餐桌服務方式？

28.I'd like to confirm your reservation.

我來確認一下您的預訂。

29.A table for two for this evening at 8: 00 for Mr.Baker. Is that right?

您為貝克先生訂的今晚8點的二人餐位，對嗎？

30.A table near the window for four at 8: 00 p.m.for

Mr.Miller.

您要為米勒先生訂今晚8點靠窗的四人餐位。

31.So it's Mr.Smith, a table of six for this evening, it's Chinese food and you're coming at 7: 00 p.m.

我再確認一下：史密斯先生、一張六人桌、中餐、晚7點到。

32.I'm sorry, the restaurant is full.

對不起，我們餐廳預訂已滿。

33.I'm afraid we're fully booked at that time.

對不起，那時間的餐位已全部訂滿。

34.Sorry, we're fully booked for today.

對不起，我們今天餐位已訂滿。

35.Would you like to make a reservation some other time?

您願意預訂其他時間的餐位嗎？

36.I'm sorry, sir. There aren't any tables left for 8: 00 p.m., but we can give you one at 8: 30 p.m.

對不起，先生，晚上8點鐘的餐位沒有了，但是8點半還有空的餐位。

37.I regret to say we can't guarantee, but we'll do our best. Hope you'll understand.

很抱歉，我們不能保證有餐位，但我們會盡力安排，希望您能理解。

38.I'm afraid we only serve lunch until 3: 00 p.m.

恐怕我們午餐只能營業到下午3點鐘。

39.The drinks are not included in the prices you quoted.

給您報的價不包括酒水。

40.The cost of the drinks will be charged separately.

酒水費用另算。

41.No, that would be extra.

不，那是額外的（不含在內，要另收費）。

42.We look forward to your coming then.

我們期待著您的光臨。

43.We look forward to having you with us.

盼望您的光臨。

# Unit 16 Receiving the Guest 接待客人

44.Do you have a reservation?

您預訂了嗎？

45.Have you got a reservation?

您有預訂嗎？

46.A table for four?

是四人桌吧？

47.Could you come with me, please?

請跟我來，好嗎？

48.This way, please.

這邊請。

49.Please step this way.

請這邊走。

50.Would you follow me, please?

請隨我來，好嗎？

51.Will this table be all right?

這張桌子可以嗎？

52.Would you like to sit near the dancing floor?

您願意靠近舞池坐嗎？

53.Where would you like to sit?

您想坐在哪兒？

54.You can sit where you like.

您可以隨便坐。

55.This is the table reserved for you. Do you like to sit here?

這是為您預留的餐桌，您願意坐這兒嗎？

56.What about that one?

那張怎麼樣？

57.I'm sorry, that table is already reserved.

對不起，那個餐桌已經有人訂了。

58.I'm sorry, the restaurant is full now. We can seat you in about 20 minutes.

對不起，餐廳現在客滿，您要等20分鐘左右。

59.I'm sorry, there isn't a table right now. I'm afraid you'll have to wait for about 20 minutes. May I have your name? we'll call you when we have a table.

對不起，現在沒有空桌了，恐怕要請您等20分鐘。請問您貴姓？一有餐位我就來叫您。

60.You can sit/have a drink/wait in the lounge if you like.We'll accommodate your party as soon as possible.

您可以在休息室坐一會／喝點飲料／稍等片刻，我們會盡快安排你們入座的。

61.Your table is ready now.

您的餐位已經準備好了。

62.Why don't you take off your coat?

您要把大衣脫了嗎？

63.Here's the menu.Please take your time. The waiter will come for your order when you're ready.

這是菜單，請慢慢點菜。等你們決定好了，服務員就會過來。

64.Here's the menu and wine list. What would you like to have?

這是菜單和酒水單，您想來點什麼？

# Unit 17 Taking Orders 點菜

65.Are you ready to order now?

您現在點菜嗎？

66.May I take your order now?

您現在可以點菜了嗎？

67.Would you like to order now?

您想現在點菜嗎？

68.Have you decided on anything?

您決定吃什麼了嗎？

69.What would you like to have, sir?

您想吃點兒什麼？

70.What would you like?

您來點兒什麼？

71.Would you like to try Chinese food?

您想吃中餐嗎？

72.What would you like to drink?

您要喝點什麼？

73.Would you like something to drink?

您想喝點什麼嗎？

74.Would you care for a drink before dinner?

您想在吃飯前喝點什麼嗎？

75.Would you like some appetizer before lunch?

飯前您想來點開胃品嗎？

76.What would you like to start with?

您想先來點什麼開胃品？

77.What dressing would you like?

您想要什麼調料？

78.What do you prefer for the dessert?

您想來點什麼甜品？

79.And to follow?

接下來呢？

80.Anything else?

還要點兒別的嗎？

81.We have prepared Chinese dishes for you.

我們為你們準備好了中餐。

82.What's the soup of today?

今天的例湯是什麼？

83.What are your chef's specialties?

今天的主廚推薦的菜是什麼？

84.What vegetables have you got?

你們有什麼蔬菜？

85.Please tell me the difference between Sichuan food and Cantonese food.

請告訴我四川菜和粵式菜的區別。

86.We specialize in Beijing cuisine.

我們主要經營北京菜。

87.We have a buffet, and you can have whatever you like for 2000 NTD.

我們有自助餐，2000元可隨便吃。

88.Everything is à la carte.

這裡只能單點。

89.What's the price of your set menu?

你們套餐的價格是多少？

90.We've got beef steak with onions today.

今天我們有洋蔥牛排。

91.Today's special is grilled chicken.

今天的特色菜是烤雞肉。

92.I would suggest that you order...

我建議您點......

93.I can recommend roast duck to you. It is very delicious.

我向您推薦烤鴨，味道特別鮮美。

94.Perhaps you might like...

也許您可以嘗一嘗......

95.I'd suggest the chef's delight—roast pigeon.

我建議您點廚師的拿手菜——烤鴿子肉。

96.How about having some...?

來點......怎麼樣？

97.Sydney oysters are good here. Would you like some?

我們這兒的雪梨牡蠣很不錯，要不要來一些？

98.How about trying some...? Maybe you'll like it.

來點......怎麼樣？也許您會喜歡吃的。

99.Why don't you try some strawberry?

來點草莓怎麼樣？

100.May I suggest...? It's very tasty.

我建議您嘗嘗......？味道很不錯。

101.I'm sure you'll enjoy it.

我保證您會喜歡的。

102.I hear it is very good.

我聽說很好吃。

103.How would you like it?

您想怎麼吃？

104.How would you like it prepared/done?

您希望怎樣做？

105.How would you like your soup served, thick or thin?

您想要什麼樣的湯，濃湯還是淡湯？

106.How would you like your steak?

牛排您要幾分熟？

107.Would you like your steak rare, medium or well done?

您希望牛排半生、適中還是熟透？

108.How would you like your salad served, with sauce or without?

您想要什麼樣的沙拉，帶調料還是不帶調料？

109.What tea would you like, green tea, black tea or jasmine tea?

您想喝什麼茶，綠茶、紅茶還是花茶？

110.Do you like your tea strong or weak?

您要濃茶還是淡茶？

111.How would you like your coffee served, black or white?

您想要什麼樣的咖啡，加不加奶？

112.I'm sorry, there're no chops left.

對不起，排骨沒有了。

113.I'm sorry, we haven't got any more lobster today. Maybe you would like to have it tomorrow.

對不起，今天的龍蝦已經賣完了，也許您可以明天再吃這道菜。

114.I'm afraid that this vegetable is not in season. Would you like to try something else?

抱歉，現在不是生長這種菜的季節，您是不是吃點別的什麼？

115.Your dining coupons doesn't include drinks.

您的餐券不含飲料。

116.I'm afraid you'll have to pay extra for that.

對不起，恐怕您得另外付費。

117.Could we have muffin instead of toast?

我們不要土司而要小鬆餅，行嗎？

118.If you want more dishes, you can order during the meal.

如果您還需要別的菜，還可以邊吃邊點。

119.We take the last orders at 10: 00.

我們10點鐘接受最後點菜。

120.This is what you've ordered.

這是您點的菜。

121.Enjoy your food.

請慢用。

122.Enjoy your meal.

請慢用。

# Unit 18 Paying the Bill 買單

123.Is everything all right?

一切都還好吧？

124.Is everything to your satisfaction?

一切都合您的意嗎？

125.How was the food?

飯菜還可以嗎？

126.Have you found everything satisfactory?

您還都滿意嗎？

127.Would you like anything else?

您還要別的什麼嗎？

128.Is there anything else?

您還要點什麼嗎？

129.Do you care for a dessert?

您想點些甜品嗎？

130.If you need anything else, just feel free to tell me.

如果您還需要別的什麼，只管告訴我好了。

131.—What's this for?

這筆是什麼（費用）？

—That's for the wine.

這是酒水錢。

132.Would you like to sign for that?

請您簽單。

133.Would you like to put it on your hotel bill?

您希望把費用匯入您的住店總帳嗎？

134.Could you sign here, please?

請在這兒簽字。

135.I'll need your signature and room number, please.

我需要您的簽字和房間號。

136.May I also have your room number, please?

我可以問一下您的房間號嗎？

137.Could you please put down your room number as well?

請將您的房間號也寫上，好嗎？

138.Thanks for coming.

感謝惠顧。

139.We look forward to your coming again.

期待著您再次光臨。

140.We're glad you've had an enjoyable meal. Welcome to our restaurant again next time.

我們很高興您用餐愉快。歡迎下次再來我們餐廳用餐。

141.It's very kind of you to say so.

您這樣說真的是太好了。

142.I'm glad you like it.

我很高興您喜歡。

143.Have a nice evening.

祝您今晚愉快。

144.Have a pleasant weekend.

祝您週末愉快！

145.Good night.

晚安。

146.Pleasant journey home.

祝您返程愉快。

147.Happy landing.

一路順風。

148.Goodbye. Thank you for coming.Please come again.

再見，謝謝光臨。歡迎再來。

# Unit 19 Bar Service 酒吧服務

149.Good evening. Welcome to Hilton Hotel.

晚上好，歡迎光臨希爾頓飯店。

150.Nice to see you.

見到您很高興。

151.What kind of beverage would you like?

您想要哪類飲料？

152.What is your pleasure, sir?

先生，您喜歡什麼？

153.What can I offer you, ladies?

女士們，我給你們上點什麼呢？

154.What can I prepare for you?

您想喝杯什麼？

155.There is no minimum charge.

沒有最低消費。

156.Your usual, sir?

和每天一樣嗎，先生？

157.Perhaps I could recommend our house wine.

也許我可以向您推薦我們自製的酒。

158.Would you like to start with a glass of beer?

您想先來一杯啤酒嗎？

159.We'd like to try some Taiwan spirits. What do you suggest?

我們想嘗嘗台灣的酒。你給我們推薦什麼？

160.What cocktails do you serve? Do you have pink lady?

你們供應哪些雞尾酒？有紅粉佳人嗎？

161.Bring us some martini on the rocks, please.

給我們加冰塊的馬丁尼酒。

162.We'd like to try the local brew.

我們想嘗嘗本地釀造的酒。

163.Bottled or draught?

是瓶裝的還是散裝的（生啤酒）？

164.Straight up or on the rocks?

加不加冰？

165.Here you are, sir.

先生，這是您要的（酒）。

166.Your beer, sir. Enjoy you drink.

先生，您要的啤酒。請慢用。

167.With or without ice, sir?

先生，請問是要加冰的還是不要冰的？

168.—I'll have a whiskey with soda water.

我想喝一杯加蘇打水的威士忌。

—Please say "when", sir.

先生，夠了您說一聲。（添加蘇打水時）

169.The same again, sir?

先生，同樣再來一杯嗎？

170.One for the road?

臨走前再喝一杯，如何？

171.The complimentary food would be on the house, of course.

贈送的食物當然是不收費的（由店家出錢）。

172.A nightcap before retiring, sir?

先生，臨睡前要喝一杯嗎？

173.How about the other half?

（剛才那杯不夠您的酒量）再來一杯，好嗎？

174.If you don't like this drink, how about...?

如果您不喜歡這個，是不是喝點......？

175.I'm not really a drinker.

我不大會喝酒。

176.I'm afraid not.

恐怕不行。

177.I'm really sorry, but you see my difficulty.

真對不起，但是希望您能體諒我。

178.Good night and pleasant dreams.

晚安，做個好夢。

179.Good night and rest well.

晚安，願您休息好。

180.Watch your step.

請小心。

181.Good night. Have a good rest.

晚安，祝您休息好。

182.Hope you'll come again tomorrow.

希望明天再來。

# Unit 20 At the Coffee Shop 咖啡廳 服務

183.What do you prefer, Chinese breakfast or continental breakfast?

您喜歡中式早餐還是西式早餐？

184.What kind of juice would you like, pineapple juice or orange juice?

您要鳳梨汁還是橘子汁？

185.How would you like your eggs cooked, boiled, fried or scrambled?

您想要什麼樣的雞蛋，煮的、煎的還是炒的？

186.Two fried eggs, sunny-side-up.

兩個煎蛋，一面煎。

187.Make it over easy.

（雞蛋）兩面稍煎一下（兩面煎軟）。

188.Make it over hard.

（雞蛋）兩面煎硬。

189.Would you like bacon, sausage or ham?

您要燻肉、香腸還是火腿？

190.Could I have croissants with my breakfast?

我早餐能來點兒牛角面包嗎？

191.So that's orange juice, two eggs sunny-side-up, croissants and coffee.

您點了橘子汁、兩個一面煎的煎蛋、牛角面包和咖啡。

192.It sounds fascinating.

聽起來太吸引人了。

193.It sounds terrific.

聽起來太棒了。

194.It's just to my taste.

（它）正對我的口胃。

195.Care for some wine?

想不想喝點葡萄酒？

196.—Anything else?

還要點兒什麼嗎？

—Not at the present moment.

暫時不要什麼了。

# Unit 21 Room Service 客房送餐服務

197.If you need anything, just feel free to call Room

Service. The number is 5.

如果需要什麼，請撥「5」與送餐服務聯繫。

198.Can we have room service 24 hours a day?

我們24小時都可以叫送餐服務嗎？

199.Would you please bring me some breakfast?

請給我們送些早餐來。

200.I'd like a snack sent up to my room.

請送一份小吃到我房間來。

201.Would you like breakfast in you room?

您要在房間裡用早餐嗎？

202.What would you like，Western or Chinese breakfast?

您想要西式早餐還是中式早餐？

203.For how many?

要訂幾份？

204.For just one person?

只要一份嗎？

205.Just one portion?

只要一份？

206.How many would you like?

您要幾份？

207.We have a good choice of drinks.

我們有多種飲料可供選擇。

208.You can choose from the menu hanging on the doorknob.

您可以按照房內菜單點菜。

209.—How long will it take?

需要多長時間送到？

—It won't take long.

很快就到。

210.It'll take 15 minutes.

需要15分鐘。

211.It will be up in a few minutes.

幾分鐘就會送到。

212.It will be up right away.

馬上就送上去。

213.I'll bring it up right away.

我馬上就給您送上去。

214.The waitress will be up shortly.

服務員一會兒就上來。

215.It won't be long.

一會兒就到。

216.Excuse me，may I put your breakfast on the table?

打擾一下，我把早餐放在桌上可以嗎？

217.Here's some fruit for you with the compliment of our manager. We apologize for the wrong dish.

這是我們經理贈送給您的水果。實在對不起，剛才上錯菜了。

218.Can you sign for it?

請您簽單。

219.I'm sorry the kitchen is closed now. We open at 11: 00 a.m.

對不起，廚房現在已熄火，上午11點才開伙。

220.We start serving at 6: 30 a.m.

我們早上6點開始服務。

221.I'm sorry, we don't serve breakfast until 6: 30 a.m.

對不起，早餐要到6點半才有。

# Unit 22 Dealing with Complaints
## 處理投訴

222.What's the problem, sir? Can I be of any assistance?

先生，出什麼問題了？我能為您做點什麼？

223.This is quite unusual. I'll look into the matter.

這很少見，我會調查些事的。

224.Sorry, I'll get you another one.

對不起，我給您換一份。

225.I'll have the chef make you another one.

我讓廚師重新為您做一份。

226.Sorry, would you like it cooked a little more?

對不起，要不要回鍋再煮一下？

227.Shall I have them cooked again?

要不要把這些菜再重做一遍？

228.I'll speak to the chef and see what he can do.

我去和廚師商量一下，看他是否能給予補救。

229.I'll have them prepare another one. Would you like some...while you are waiting?

我去讓他們再做一份，在等的同時您是不是先吃點......？

230.Would you like me to send it back?

您要我把它送回去嗎？

231.Sorry, I'll change it for you at once.

對不起，我馬上為您換。

232.I'm terribly sorry. I can offer you something else if you'd like; that'll be on the house, of course.

非常抱歉。如果您願意，我們可以給您上點別的菜，這當然算是本店免費招待的。

233.Would you like to try something else? With our compliments, of course.

您想不想吃點別的？這當然算是我們餐廳的小小敬意。

234.I can offer you some..., compliments of the chef.

我給您上點兒......，作為我們廚師對您的敬意。

235.It takes quite a while to prepare.

做這道菜要花些時間。

236.I'll check your order with the chef immediately.

我馬上去問廚師，看您的菜做好沒有。

237.I'm sorry, please excuse her. We're very busy today.

對不起，請原諒她。我們今天實在太忙了。

238.I'm sorry, we're short of help today. Would you like to have a drink first?

對不起，我們今天人手少。您是不是先喝點兒什麼？

239.Please accept my apology on behalf of the hotel/restaurant.

請接受我代表飯店 / 餐廳的道歉。

240.I'm sure everything will be right again next time you come.

我保證您下次再來時一切都會好的。

# Part Four Convention and Exhibition Center 會展中心

# Unit 23 Convention 會議

1.I'm Jane, director of Convention Sales Dept.

我是珍，會議銷售部主任。

2.I'm here to discuss with you about holding a meeting at your property.

我今天來是要和您討論一下在貴飯店舉行一個會議的事宜。

3.What meeting is it?

請問是什麼會議？

4.Can I see the name list of the attendees?

我能看一下出席者的名單嗎？

5.How many participants will there be?

請問有多少人參會？

6.There are 120 attendees. I think our medium-sized meeting room can serve your purpose.

共有120名與會者，我想我們的中型會議廳可以滿足您的需求。

7.Here are the convention brochures showing the details about meeting facilities.

這是會議服務宣傳冊，裡面有關於會議設備的詳細介紹。

8.Do you have sufficient number of breakout rooms? We have several seminars after the plenary session.

你們有足夠多的分組討論會議室嗎？我們在全體會議後要開幾個研討會。

9.We'll let you know by fax once we've decided.

一旦決定下來，我們會發傳真通知您。

10.This meeting hall can accommodate about 400 people.

這個會議大廳可容納400人。

11.The center of the multi-purpose hall is the main

conference auditorium seating 400.

多功能廳中央是主會場，可容納400人。

12.Our conference hall is multi-purpose.

我們的會議廳是多功能廳。

13.We have a fully-equipped convention center that provides complete secretarial service.

我們會議中心設備齊全，提供全套秘書服務。

14.We have all the state-of-the-art audio-visual equipment.

我們擁有全套一流的視聽設備。

15.And we have simultaneous translation system.

我們有同聲傳譯系統。

16.We have some brand-new imported equipment.

我們有幾種全新的進口設備。

17.You can hire our nightclub for private use.

夜總會你們也可以租用。

18.I'll send you a support facility list with a price list by fax.

我會把配套設備清單和價目表傳真給您。

19.So you'd like to reserve our conference room for 3 days together with an overhead projector.

我來確認一下，您要預訂我們的會議室開三天會，並需要一臺投影機。

20.Here is the rental rate list for equipment and personnel for the convention.

這是會議設備租金單和會議服務員名單。

21.Perhaps we could just test out the microphone and amplifier.

我們還是試一試麥克風和擴音器。

22.I'll take you to the auditorium and we can both check the equipment on the spot.

我這就帶您去會議廳，現場檢查一下會議設備。

23.When will the pre-conference meeting be held?

會前會議什麼時候開？

24.The convention service manager is demonstrating the electronically operated furniture and AVs (audio-visuals)

會議服務經理正在示範控制設備和視聽設備。

25.The center can comfortably seat 400 people.And this is the 800-square-meter center stage.

這個中心可輕鬆容納400位來賓。這是800平方米的中央舞臺。

26.There is to be an awards ceremony. We need raised tiers for those prizewinners.

我們有一個頒獎儀式，需要給那些獲獎者準備升降臺。

27.Will there be any special dietary requirement?

餐飲方面有什麼特別要求嗎？

28.Our restaurant caters for various religions.

我們餐廳可為信仰不同宗教的人士提供餐飲。

29.We have a good selection of vegetarian dishes.

我們的素食菜餚品種多樣。

30.How would you like the banquet to be served?

您想要什麼樣的宴會服務方式？

31.What about the minimum you charge for each attendee?

每位與會者最低費用是多少？

32.400 NTD each for one day.

每人每天400元。

33.As for the menu choice, We'd like the routine entrée and chef's choice for the two banquets on the first day and the last day respectively. Buffets are for other meals on other days.

至於菜單，我們想第一天和最後一天的兩個宴會分別用常規的主菜搭配主廚推薦菜，其他幾天用自助餐。

34.Here is your meeting badge and meeting packet.

這是您的參會證件和會議資料袋。

35.The packet contains a layout of the hotel, a map of downtown Shanghai, nearby restaurant information and other related items.

資料袋裡有一張飯店平面圖、一張上海商業區地圖，還有附近

餐館訊息及其他相關物品。

36.By the way, where is the preparation area? I need to review my audio-visual presentation.

順便問一下，發言準備區在哪兒？我想去再瀏覽一下我的多媒體發言稿。

37.When and where does the plenary session begin?

全體會議什麼時候在哪兒召開？

38.In the Peony Conference Hall it starts at 8: 30 a.m.

上午8點半在牡丹會議廳。

39.We'll put the extra expenses of refreshing on your account.

我們要將額外的點心飲料費用匯入您的總帳。

40.Are you sure all rented equipment is included in the inventory list?

您確信所有被租用的設備都列在物品清單上了嗎？

41.Our personnel will collect all the signs and return them to you.

我們的服務員會收集所有的標誌牌，然後交還給你們。

42.There are 5 no-shows and 4 early departures.

有5位應與會者未到，有4位早退。

43.The final account shall be settled by these supporting vouchers.

最終帳目將根據這些有效憑證計算。

44.We look forward to meeting you for the next convention.

我們期待下次會議能再與您合作。

# Unit 24 Exhibition 展覽

45.I know you have received the outline we sent to you for the coming exhibition. And I want to confirm the date in person.

我知道您收到了我們寄給您的有關展覽日程表。今天我想與您當面確認一下展覽日期。

46.The exhibition is to be held on the 26th and 27th, for two days.

展覽將於26日、27日兩天舉行。

47.What's the capacity of your exhibition hall? We are expecting an attendance of 400 at a time.

你們的展廳能容納多少人？我們預計一次有400 人參觀。

48.Our exhibition hall can hold 800 people.

我們的展廳能容納800人。

49.Do you have any special requirement about the decoration of the exhibition hall?

你們對展廳裝飾有何特別要求？

50.Do you need aisle carpet to cover the ground?

需要在過道鋪紅地毯嗎？

51.Do you also need flowers and plants to decorate the hall?

還需要鮮花和盆景點綴展廳嗎？

52.The flowers and plants can help to create friendly and harmonious atmosphere for the show. Be sure to make them fresh and fragrant.

鮮花和綠植有助於營造友好和諧的氣氛，但一定要確保新鮮和芳香。

53.According to the schedule，the exhibits are arriving this afternoon. I wonder whether your staff are ready for unpacking?

按計劃，展品今天下午到，你們的職員做好拆包準備了吧？

54.We have served a dozen such exhibitions before. Our unpacking staff are professionals.

我們有為十幾個這樣的展覽服務的經驗，我們擁有專業的拆包人員。

55.These exhibits are glassware. You can't be too careful in moving them.

這些展品是玻璃製品，搬動時務必多加小心。

56.Do you have sufficient storage area for the large container boxes?

你們有足夠大的儲藏區域存放貨櫃嗎？

57.There is a 1600-square-meter house right beside the

exhibition hall. It can house 20 large container boxes at a time.

在展廳旁邊有一間1600平方米的平房，一次能容納20個貨櫃。

58.How are you getting along with the setting-up of booths?

展位搭建進展怎麼樣了？

59.We have just finished the space assignment.

展位剛剛分配完畢。

60.The island booth takes up so much space. What about peninsula booth? In that case, more space is saved.

島形展位占據的容間較多，半島形展位怎麼樣？這樣可以節省更多空間。

61.Where do you plan to locate the show office?

您打算把展覽辦公室放在哪裡？

62.Better put it near the entrance.

在靠近入口處好一些。

63.How do you like the decorating done?

您想怎麼裝飾？

64.Because this is the tabletop display, we wish there to be good draping.

因為這是臺面展示，我們希望用帶垂邊的布藝裝飾臺面。

65.Everything shall be ready tomorrow morning. Would you come and check then?

明天下午一切都將準備完畢，屆時請您來檢查一下。

66.Our company delivered the exhibits later than schedule. Could you ask your staff to unload the exhibits and move in right away?

我們公司運送展品比計劃晚了些，請你們的職員趕快把展品卸下搬進展廳，好嗎？

67.What is the number of the exhibits?

有多少件展品？

68.What kind of exhibits are they?

是什麼類型的展品？

69.They are some glassware and porcelain. They must be handled with care.

是一些玻璃器具和瓷器，搬運時一定多加小心。

70.Could you help us unpack the exhibits?

你們能幫我們拆包嗎？

71.How was the exhibits packed?

展品是如何包裝的？

72.I'm the dispatcher. What can I do for you?

我是裝卸工，有何吩咐？

73.Our company has finished dismantling.

我們公司已拆除完展臺。

74.We also have some exhibits left.Because we want to present them to the municipal Art Gallery for their long-standing help.

有一些展品我們要留下來，我們要把它們贈送給貴市藝術館，以感謝他們多年來對我們的支持。

75.Our convention center also serves as an exhibition hall.

我們的會議中心也可用作展廳。

76.Stands can be laid out in regular rows along gangways.

展臺可沿過道規則排列。

77.For this type of exhibits, we shall leave 2.5-meter aisles.

展覽這種展品要留2.5米寬的過道。

78.Visitor circulation in the hall is planned on a simple grid arrangement.

觀覽通道成方格狀安排。

79.Uniform signposting, together with the use of identifying symbols, numbers and color codes, is essential for orientation and direction to a particular area.

為了引導參展者到某一指定區域，使用統一路標和識別符號、數字及色標至關重要。

80.We offer to both visitors and exhibitors a choice of food and beverage service.

我們為參展者和辦展者提供餐飲服務。

81.We provide separate F & B service module in each hall.

每個廳都有獨立的餐飲服務區域。

82.Portable counters are provided for snack and

refreshment services.

有流動櫃臺提供小吃和飲料售賣服務。

83.There is an additional toilet area for the disabled.

我們有殘疾人專用衛生間。

84.If overseas visitors and exhibitors want to get travel information, they may go to the travel desk in the public counters.

海外參展者和辦展者如想瞭解旅遊訊息，可到設在公眾服務處的旅遊服務臺諮詢。

85.Would it be more appropriate to fix fluorescent lighting?

用螢光燈可能會更好。

86.I think the hall should be very luminous with glare of light, because this is a high-tech products show.

這是一個高科技產品展覽會，我想用強光照射使展廳明亮些會比較好。

87.I wonder if you'd prefer soft diffused natural lighting for the work of art.

對於這些藝術品，我想知道您是否願意用柔和散射的自然光呢？

88.For this particular delicate material, the temperature can be adjusted to 21 degrees centigrade.

對於這種易損的特殊材料，可以將溫度調到21度。

89.Carpet strips and acoustic panels have been prepared

to reduce excessive noise levels.

地毯條和隔音板準備用來減少過量的噪音。

# Part Five Health & Recreation Center 康樂中心

## Unit 25 Health Center 健身中心

Ⅰ.Bowling

保齡球

1.Are there any alleys availalale at the moment?

現在有空的球道嗎？

2.VIP alley or regular alley，sir?

先生，您要貴賓球道還是普通球道？

3.Let me take the bowling shoes for you. What size?

我給您拿保齡球專用鞋，您穿幾號？

4.Size 41.

41號。

5.How many games would you like to play?

你們要玩多少局？

6.What size bowling balls would you like, sir?

先生，你們要幾磅的球？

7.We'd like 14-pound balls.

我們要14磅的球。

8.Please show me your deposit receipt, sir.

先生，請出示押金收據。

II.At the Hair Saloon

在美髮沙龍

9.Now it's your turn, sir. This way, please. I'll give you a shampoo first.

先生，現在該您了。請這邊來，我先給您洗一下頭。

10.Wet or dry shampoo, sir?

先生，要濕洗還是乾洗？

11.How would you like your hair done?

您想要什麼髮型？

12.Not too short on the forehead, not so much off at the back.

前額不要太短，後面稍剪一下就行了

13.Do you want a shave?

您要修臉嗎？

14.I'd like you to trim my beard.

把鬍子刮一下。

15.Some hair tonic would be good to your hair.

上一些潤髮劑對您的頭髮會有好處。

16.Should I do the parting on the right side or left side?

頭髮偏左分還是偏右分？

17.Your hair is growing thin, sir.

先生，您的頭髮掉了不少。

18.We have one type of hair-restorer. I suggest that you give it a try.

本店有一種專治脫髮的藥水，您不妨試一試。

19.My hair is growing too gray. I want it dyed.

我的白髮不少，我想染一下。

20.What color do you prefer?

您想染成什麼顏色？

21.Do you want me to trim your moustache?

鬍鬚要不要修一修？

22.Does the haircut suit you, sir?

這樣可以嗎，先生？

23.Please have a look in the mirror. Is it all right?

請您照照鏡子，可以嗎？

24.Are you planning to get a manicure later?

您打算過會兒修修指甲嗎？

III.Sauna-Bathing

桑拿浴

25.We also offer massage on call.

我們的按摩師隨叫隨到。

26.Want a Finnish Sauna.

我想選芬蘭浴。

27.What's the temperature of the sauna room. When is the dry steam given off?

桑拿室的溫度怎麼樣？什麼時候放乾蒸汽？

28.Would you like some ice water and icy face towel?

您想要冰水和涼毛巾嗎？

29.Don't you want to cool off under a shower or have a quick swim?

您不想沖個淋浴或游個泳來涼快涼快嗎？

30.How are you feeling now?

現在感覺怎麼樣？

IV.Body-Building

健身活動

31.Welcome to the gym. The number of your locker, please?

歡迎來到健身中心。請問您的鎖櫃鑰匙號碼？

32.Wow, you have a lot of apparatus here.

哇，你們的體育器材不少啊。

33.Basically there are two types: the ones for aerobics and the ones for strengthening your muscles.

這裡的器材基本分兩類：一類用作有氧健身，另一類用來鍛鍊肌肉。

34.I'll try to run on the treadmill.

我想試試跑步機。

35.The gym is very modern.

這個健身房很現代化。

36.The barbell is too heavy. Try the dumbbell.

槓鈴太重，試試啞鈴吧。

37.You can also play badminton here.

您還可以在這兒打羽毛球。

38.I said I'd like my shoes polished.

我剛才說希望能把我的鞋子擦一擦。

39.Your polished shoes were put in the closet.

擦好了，給您放在櫃子裡了。

Ⅴ.Swimming Pool

室內泳

40.The swimming suits, caps and goggles are on sale today.

泳衣、泳帽和泳鏡今天都減價銷售。

41.May I have a complete set of them?

給我來一套吧。

42.We change the water of the indoor swimming pool every other day.

室內游泳池每隔一天換一次水。

43.The temperature in the pool today is about 21 degrees centigrade.

今天泳池的溫度是21攝氏度。

44.I'm afraid the water is too cold in such cold weather.

今兒天冷，水恐怕也很涼。

45.Don't worry. Ours is a heated swimming pool. The temperature is as high as 28 degrees centigrade.

別擔心，我們的泳池是溫水游泳池，水溫高達 28 攝氏度。

46.You may have a dip in our heated swimming pool.

您可以去溫水池泡一泡。

47.If you don't swim well, you can swim in the shallow area. It is a half meter to two meters deep.

如果您不怎麼會游，可以到淺水區，深度是0.5米至2米。

48.If you feel tired, you may relax with soft drinks at the pool side bar.

如果覺得累了，您可以在池邊的水吧休息一下，喝點軟飲料。

49.For staying guest, they're free of charge.

這些對住店客人是免費的。

50.We've kick board and buoy on loan. You'd better start with the shallow area.

我們有踢水板和游泳圈供出租。您最好從淺水區開始。

51.What's the use of the kick board?

踢水板有什麼用？

52.Just hold it in your hands, and kick. In this way, you can learn swimming quickly.

把踢水板抓在手中，然後踏水，這樣練你很快就學會了。

53.Do you have a female coach here?

你們這兒有女教練嗎？

54.We have an experienced one. She'll make you a great swimmer in the shortest possible time.

我們有一個很有經驗的教練，她可以在最短的時間內讓您成為

游泳高手。

55.The clean towels are putting on the hanger in the center of the bathroom.

乾淨毛巾掛在浴室中央的衣架上。

56.Here's the key to the locker.

這是您鎖櫃的鑰匙。

# Unit 26 Recreation Center 娛樂中心

57.It's the first time I've come to the nightclub. What can we expect to enioy here?

我是第一次來夜總會，這兒都有哪些娛樂和服務項目？

58.A variety of things.You can dine, wine and enjoy good floor show.

項目很多，您可以用餐、喝酒，還可以欣賞各種表演。

59.How much do you charge for it?

怎麼收費？

60.You may dance till 2: 00 a.m. to two bands.

您可以伴著兩個樂隊一直跳到凌晨兩點鐘。

61.The floor show changes every week.

演出節目每週更換。

62.Which do you prefer, VIP or regular table?

您喜歡包廂還是大廳？

63.What do you charge for this VIP room?

這個包廂怎麼收費？

64.1500 NTD per hour, not including drinks and dry snacks.

每小時1500元，不包括飲料和小吃。

65.Take your seat, please. And your time starts at 6: 30 p.m.

請坐，你們的時間從下午6點半開始。

66.What's the song being played?

正在播放的是什麼曲子？

67.It's called The Butterfly Lovers, a Chinese folk music telling a story about the Chinese Romeo and Juliet—Liang Shanbo and Zhu Yingtai.

這首曲子叫「化蝶」，是一首中國民間樂曲，講述的是一個關於中國的羅密歐和朱麗葉——梁山伯與祝英臺的愛情故事。

68.It's moving and melodious.

真是悅耳動聽。

69.Your time ends at 7: 30 p.m., one hour in all.

你們的結束時間是晚7點半，共一個小時。

70.This is the drink list and that is the song list.

這是飲品單，那是點歌單。

71.We have the performance of dance, singing, fashion

show and showmanship, including the lucky draw. I hope you'll join us.

我們這裡有舞蹈表演、唱歌、時裝表演，還有抽獎活動，歡迎您的參與。

72.We have Heineken, Carlsberg and Blue Ribbon.

我們的啤酒有荷蘭的喜力、丹麥的嘉士伯以及美國的藍帶。

73.The music has started. It's a slow waltz.

音樂開始了，這是慢華爾茲。

74.There is an average charge of 300 NTD per person.

先生，每人300元。

75.The minimum charge is 400 NTD for each, including drinks.

每位最低消費400元，含飲料。

76.Please wait a minute. When your turn comes, the D.J. will announce through the microphone.

請稍等，輪到您時，調音師會透過麥克風叫您。

77.Can I take your song order?

可以點歌了嗎？

78.Attention, please. Next is an English song. Mrs.Green at Table 6 is welcome to the stage.

各位來賓，下面是一首英文歌曲，有請6 號桌的格林夫人上來為大家演唱。

79.Do you want to sit at a table or at the bar?

您要一個桌位還是靠吧臺坐？

80.Would you please let me put your coat at the cloakroom?

讓我把您的外套存放在衣帽間裡吧。

81.This is the number plate to your coat.

這是您取衣服的號牌。

82.What do you care for as drinks?

您來點什麼飲料？

83.What types of dance are there tonight?

今晚都有什麼舞蹈？

84.There are disco, tango, and to finish with rock-and-roll.

有迪斯科、探戈，最後以搖滾結束。

85.Do you need a partner?

您需要舞伴嗎？

86.That's waltz. It's a beautiful dance. Will you have a try?

這是一曲優美的華爾滋，您要跳一曲嗎？

87.I'm fond of sitting and watching people dance.

我喜歡坐著看別人跳。

88.We'd like to play bridge. Is there any table available?

我們想玩橋牌，有空桌子嗎？

89.This way, please. Is this room all right?

這邊請。這個房間如何？

90.May I ask if you could recommend to us a chief coach?

我想問一下，你能為我們推薦一位主教練嗎？

91.This is our chief coach, Ms Li. She will help you all through the game.

這是我們的主教練，李女士，她將在整個遊戲中幫助你們。

92.Please don't forget to carry the belongings with you. Good night!

請別忘了拿上你們的東西。晚安！

93.What do you prefer, net chatting, net entertainment, net games, E-mail or net shopping?

您要哪種上網服務，網上聊天、網上娛樂、在線遊戲、電子郵件還是網上購物？

94.Would you please feel free to call me if you need to download files?

您要想下載文檔，請隨時叫我。

# Appendix 附錄

# Appendix I 535 Classified Basic English Words for Hotel Service
## 飯店服務英語基本分類詞彙535個

Countries（國名，10）

| America | 美國 |
|---------|------|
| Canada | 加拿大 |
| China | 中國 |
| England | 英國 |
| France | 法國 |
| Germany | 德國 |
| Italy | 義大利 |
| Japan | 日本 |
| Singapore | 新加坡 |
| Thailand | 泰國 |

Cities（城市名，5）

| Hong Kong | 香港 |
|-----------|------|
| London | 倫敦 |
| Taipei | 台北 |
| New York | 紐約 |
| Paris | 巴黎 |

Week（星期，7）

| | |
|---|---|
| Monday | 星期一 |
| Tuesday | 星期二 |
| Wednesday | 星期三 |
| Thursday | 星期四 |
| Friday | 星期五 |
| Saturday | 星期六 |
| Sunday | 星期日 |

Seasons（季節，4）

| | |
|---|---|
| spring | 春季 |
| summer | 夏季 |
| autumn/fall | 秋季 |
| winter | 冬季 |

Months（月份，12）

| | |
|---|---|
| January | 一月 |
| February | 二月 |
| March | 三月 |
| April | 四月 |
| May | 五月 |
| June | 六月 |
| July | 七月 |

| | |
|---|---|
| August | 八月 |
| September | 九月 |
| October | 十月 |
| November | 十一月 |
| December | 十二月 |
| Time（時間‧30） | |
| second | 秒 |
| minuite | 分鐘 |
| quarter | 一刻鐘 |
| half an hour | 半小時 |
| hour | 小時 |
| morning | 上午 |
| noon | 中午 |
| afternoon | 下午 |
| evening | 晚上 |
| night | 夜晚 |
| day | 白天；天 |
| date | 日期 |
| today | 今天 |
| yesterday | 昨天 |
| the day before yesterday | 前天 |

| | |
|---|---|
| tomorrow | 明天 |
| the day after tomorrow | 後天 |
| week | 週 |
| weekend | 週末 |
| last week | 上週 |
| next week | 下週 |
| month | 月 |
| quarter | 季度，三個月 |
| season | 季節 |
| half a year | 半年 |
| year | 年 |
| last year | 去年 |
| next year | 明年 |
| decade | 十年 |
| centennial | 一百（週）年 |

Directions（方向，8）

| | |
|---|---|
| east | 東 |
| north | 北 |
| northeast | 東北 |
| northwest | 西北 |
| south | 南 |

| | |
|---|---|
| southeast | 東南 |
| southwest | 西南 |
| west | 西 |

Hotel（飯店，5）

| | |
|---|---|
| guest house | 賓館；招待所 |
| hostel | 旅舍 |
| hotel | 飯店 |
| inn | 旅店 |
| motel | 汽車旅館 |

Hotel Departments（飯店部門，11）

| | |
|---|---|
| Accounting Department | 財務部 |
| Business Center | 商務中心 |
| Engineering Department | 工程部 |
| Food & Beverage Department | 餐飲部 |
| Front Office | 客務部 |
| Health & Recreation Center | 康樂中心 |
| Housekeeping Department | 客房部 |
| Human Resources Department | 人力資源部 |
| Public Relations Department | 公關部 |
| Sales & Marketing Department | 銷售部 |
| Training Section | 培訓部 |

Positions in the Hotel（飯店工作職位，14）

| | |
|---|---|
| assistant manager | 大堂副理 |
| bell captain | 大堂領班 |
| bellboy | 行李員 |
| bartender | 酒吧服務員 |
| cashier | 收銀員 |
| chamber maid | 客房服務員 |
| doorman | 門童 |
| general manager | 總經理 |
| operator | 接線員 |
| receptionist | 櫃臺服務員 |
| repairman | 維修工 |
| supervisor | 主管 |
| waiter | 男服務員 |
| waitress | 女服務員 |

Careers（職業，10）

| | |
|---|---|
| baker | 麵包師 |
| barber | 理髮師 |
| chef | 廚師 |
| doctor | 醫生 |
| driver | 司機 |

| | |
|---|---|
| hairdresser | 高級美髮師（尤指為女士服務的） |
| lawyer | 律師 |
| nurse | 護士 |
| tour guide | 導遊 |
| trainer | 培訓師 |

Colors（顏色，12）

| | |
|---|---|
| black | 黑色 |
| blue | 藍色 |
| dark brown | 深褐色 |
| gray | 灰色 |
| green | 綠色 |
| light blue | 淡藍色 |
| orange | 橘紅色 |
| pink | 粉紅色 |
| purple | 紫色 |
| red | 紅色 |
| white | 白色 |
| yellow | 黃色 |

Drinks（飲料，16）

| | |
|---|---|
| black coffee | 黑咖啡（不加奶） |
| black tea | 紅茶 |

| | |
|---|---|
| brandy | 白蘭地 |
| cocktail | 雞尾酒 |
| green tea | 綠茶 |
| ice cube | 冰塊 |
| iced water | 冰水 |
| jasmine tea | 茉莉花茶 |
| juice | 果汁 |
| lemonade | 檸檬水 |
| milk | 牛奶 |
| mineral water | 礦泉水 |
| sprite | 雪碧 |
| whisky | 威士忌 |
| white coffee | 加奶的咖啡 |
| yogurt | 優格 |

Fruits（水果‧12）

| | |
|---|---|
| apple | 蘋果 |
| banana | 香蕉 |
| cherry | 櫻桃 |
| coconut | 椰子 |
| Hami melon (honeydew melon) | 哈密瓜 |
| lemon | 檸檬 |

| | |
|---|---|
| lychee | 荔枝 |
| peach | 桃 |
| pear | 梨 |
| strawberry | 草莓 |
| sugarcane | 甘蔗 |
| water melon | 西瓜 |
| Seasoning（調味品，11） | |
| chilli | 紅辣椒 |
| Chinese onion | 大蔥 |
| garlic | 大蒜 |
| ginger | 姜 |
| gourmet powder | 味精 |
| olive oil | 橄欖油 |
| pepper | 胡椒 |
| salt | 鹽 |
| soy sauce | 醬油 |
| sugar | 糖 |
| vinegar | 醋 |
| Baggage（箱包行李，8） | |
| luggage/baggage | 行李 |
| suitcase | 手提箱 |

| traveling bag | 旅行包 |
| shoulder bag | 肩包；背包 |
| handbag | （女用）手提包 |
| wallet | 錢夾 |
| trunk | 箱子；汽車後備箱 |
| backpack | 背包 |

## Clothing and Other Personal Items

（衣物及其他個人用品，27）

| battery | 電池 |
| camera | 照相機 |
| comb | 梳子 |
| dress | 女服 |
| jacket | 夾克衫 |
| jeans | 牛仔褲 |
| knife | 小刀 |
| leather shoes | 皮鞋 |
| lighter | 打火機 |
| make-up case | 化妝盒 |
| nail-clippers | 指甲刀 |
| note-pad | 記事本 |
| overcoat | 外套大衣 |

| | |
|---|---|
| pajamas | 睡衣 |
| pants | 褲子 |
| razor | 刮鬍刀 |
| safe pin | 別針 |
| scissors | 剪刀 |
| shorts | 短褲 |
| shirt | 襯衫 |
| skirt | 裙子 |
| socks | 短襪 |
| stockings | 長襪 |
| suit | 西服 |
| sweater | 毛衣 |
| underwear | 內衣褲 |
| uniform | 制服 |

Food（食品，37）

| | |
|---|---|
| afternoon tea | 下午茶 |
| appetizer | 開胃品（如，少量的酒） |
| bacon | 燻肉 |
| beef | 牛肉 |
| Beijing Roast Duck | 北京烤鴨 |
| bread | 麵包 |

| | |
|---|---|
| bun | 小而圓的甜麵包 |
| butter | 黃油 |
| cabbage | 圓白菜；捲心菜 |
| cheese | 奶酪 |
| chicken | 雞肉 |
| chip | 薯片 |
| chocolate | 巧克力 |
| dessert | 甜點 |
| duck | 鴨 |
| fish | 魚 |
| ham | 火腿 |
| hamburger | 漢堡 |
| hot dog | 熱狗 |
| jam | 果醬 |
| ketchup | 番茄醬 |
| local flavor | 地方風味 |
| main course | 主菜 |
| mushroom | 蘑菇 |
| mutton | 羊肉 |
| noodle | 麵條 |
| pie | 餡餅 |

| | |
|---|---|
| pizza | 比薩 |
| pork | 豬肉 |
| porridge | 麥片粥 |
| potato | 馬鈴薯 |
| rice gruel | 稀飯 |
| sausage | 香腸 |
| snack | 小吃 |
| steak | 牛排 |
| steamed bun | 饅頭 |
| steamed stuffed bun | 包子 |

## Sports（運動項目，8）

| | |
|---|---|
| basketball | 籃球 |
| billiard | 撞球 |
| bowling | 保齡球 |
| football/soccer | 足球 |
| golf | 高爾夫球 |
| table tennis | 乒乓球 |
| tennis | 網球 |
| swimming | 游泳 |

## Types of Guest Rooms（客房類型，9）

| | |
|---|---|
| adjoining room | 連通房 |

| | |
|---|---|
| deluxe suite | 豪華套房 |
| double room | 大床房 |
| presidential suite | 總統套房 |
| single room | 單人房 |
| standard room | 標準房 |
| suite | 套房 |
| triple room | 三人房 |
| twin-bed room | 雙床房 |

Items and Facilities in Guest Room（客房用品和設備35）

| | |
|---|---|
| air-conditioner | 空調 |
| bath cap | 浴帽 |
| bath curtain | 浴簾 |
| bath foam | 沐浴液 |
| bathroom | 浴室 |
| bathtub | 浴缸 |
| bed sheet | 床單 |
| bed spread | 床罩 |
| bulb | 電燈泡 |
| closet | 壁櫥 |
| cooling | 冷氣 |
| curtain | 窗簾 |

| | |
|---|---|
| faucet | 水龍頭 |
| fridge | 冰箱 |
| heating | 暖氣 |
| hair conditioner | 護髮乳 |
| hanger | 衣架 |
| knob | 把手 |
| laundry bag | 洗衣袋 |
| lotion | 洗液，潔膚液，沐浴乳 |
| mirror | 鏡子 |
| pillow | 枕頭 |
| plug | 插頭 |
| quilt | 被子 |
| restroom | 休息室 |
| shampoo | 洗髮水 |
| sink | 洗手池；水槽 |
| soap | 香皂 |
| tap | 水龍頭 |
| toilet | 廁所 |
| toothbrush | 牙刷 |
| toothpaste | 牙膏 |
| towel | 毛巾 |

| | |
|---|---|
| wardrobe | 衣櫥；衣櫃 |
| washbasin | 臉盆 |

Jewelry（首飾，7）

| | |
|---|---|
| earring | 耳環 |
| brooch | 胸針 |
| bracelet | 手鐲 |
| jewel | 寶石；珠寶 |
| necklace | 項鏈 |
| ring | 戒指 |
| wedding ring | 結婚戒指 |

Transportation（交通，13）

| | |
|---|---|
| airline/airways | 航空公司 |
| airport | 機場 |
| bus stop | 公共汽車站 |
| by air | 乘飛機 |
| by land | 經由陸路 |
| by water | 經由水路 |
| plane | 飛機 |
| public transportation | 公共交通 |
| ship | 輪船 |
| subway/tube/underground | 地鐵（捷運） |

| | |
|---|---|
| taxi | 計程車 |
| terminal | 終點站 |
| train station | 火車站 |
| Verbs（常用動詞，61） | |
| accept | 接受 |
| answer | 回答 |
| arrange | 安排 |
| arrive | 到達 |
| bake | 烤；烘 |
| bring | 帶來 |
| carry | 攜帶 |
| charge | 收（費）；要（價） |
| collect | 收集 |
| confirm | 確認 |
| copy | 複印（影印） |
| delay | 耽誤 |
| enjoy | 喜歡 |
| follow | 跟隨 |
| forget | 忘記 |
| get off | 下車 |
| get on | 上車 |

| | |
|---|---|
| get up | 起床 |
| go straight | 直走 |
| hold on | 別掛電話 |
| hope | 希望 |
| improve | 改善 |
| increase | 增加 |
| jog | 慢跑 |
| join | 參加 |
| knock | 敲（門） |
| lack | 缺乏 |
| laugh | 笑 |
| leave | 離開 |
| lose | 丟失 |
| make a mistake | 犯錯 |
| make bed | 整理床鋪 |
| manage | 管理 |
| miss | 想念；錯過 |
| pass | 傳遞 |
| recite | 背誦 |
| refuse | 拒絕 |
| register | 登記 |

| | |
|---|---|
| remember | 記得；想起 |
| reserve | 預訂 |
| serve | 為......服務；招待 （顧客等）；端上，擺出（飯菜等） |
| shout | 呼喊 |
| show | 出示 |
| sign | 簽（名） |
| smile | 微笑 |
| stay | 暫住 |
| translate | 翻譯 |
| turn down | 關小 |
| turn left | 左轉 |
| turn off | 關 |
| turn on | 開 |
| turn up | 開大 |
| understand | 明白 |
| visit | 訪問 |
| wait | 等待 |
| wake up | 醒來 |
| walk | 步行 |
| wash | 洗 |
| wear | 穿 |

| | |
|---|---|
| welcome | 歡迎 |
| wish | 希望 |

## Adjectives（常用形容詞，45）

| | |
|---|---|
| afraid | 害怕的 |
| angry | 生氣的 |
| available | 可使用的 |
| careful | 小心的 |
| cheap | 便宜的 |
| clean | 乾淨的 |
| comfortable | 舒適的 |
| correct | 正確的 |
| dear | 昂貴的 |
| delicious | 美味的 |
| dirty | 髒的 |
| dry | 乾的 |
| excellent | 優秀的 |
| foreign | 外國的 |
| free | 自由的 |
| fresh | 新鮮的 |
| healthy | 健康的 |
| homesick | 想家的 |

| | |
|---|---|
| hopeful | 有希望的 |
| hopeless | 沒有希望的 |
| hungry | 餓的 |
| ill-mannered | 態度惡劣的 |
| important | 重要的 |
| indoor | 室內的 |
| local | 當地的 |
| lonely | 寂寞的 |
| lucky | 幸運的 |
| noisy | 喧鬧的，嘈雜的 |
| outdoor | 戶外的，室外的 |
| overweight | 超重的 |
| quiet | 安靜的 |
| sick | 生病的 |
| sleepy | 瞌睡兮兮的 |
| slippery | 滑的 |
| spare | 備用的；多餘的；空閒的 |
| spicy | 辣的 |
| thin | 瘦的 |
| thirsty | 渴的 |
| tidy | 整潔的 |

| | |
|---|---|
| tired | 累的 |
| total | 總共 |
| typical | 典型的 |
| well-mannered | 有禮貌的 |
| wet | 濕的 |
| wrong | 錯誤的 |

## Others（其他‧118）

| | |
|---|---|
| between | 在......之間 |
| bill | 帳單 |
| booklet | 小冊子 |
| bottle | 瓶子 |
| brand | 商標；牌子 |
| brunch | 早午餐 |
| business | 商業；生意 |
| cash | 現金 |
| cent | 分 |
| check | 支票 |
| Christmas | 聖誕節 |
| credit card | 信用卡 |
| dining hall | 餐廳 |
| dinner | 正餐；宴會 |

| | |
|---|---|
| disc/disk | 磁盤；唱片 |
| dish | （一道）菜 |
| dollar | 美元 |
| drawer | 抽屜 |
| dry clean | 乾洗 |
| elevator/lift | 電梯 |
| E-mail | 電子郵件 |
| entrance | 入口 |
| exit | 出口 |
| facility | (pl.) 設備 |
| fan | 風扇；狂熱愛好者，迷 |
| fax | 傳真 |
| female | 女性（的） |
| first class | 一等艙 |
| fitness center | 健身中心 |
| floor | 樓層 |
| flour | 麵粉 |
| flower | 花 |
| fork | 叉子 |
| form | 表格 |
| friend | 朋友 |

| | |
|---|---|
| future | 將來 |
| greeting | 問候 |
| group guest | 團隊客人 |
| gym | 體育館 |
| health club | 健身俱樂部 |
| habit | 習慣 |
| hairstyle | 髮型 |
| handkerchief | 手帕 |
| holiday | 假日 |
| homeland | 家鄉 |
| IDD call | 國際直撥電話 |
| Internet | 互聯網 |
| jar | 罐子 |
| journey | 旅行 |
| kid | 小孩 |
| kitchen | 廚房 |
| kite | 風箏 |
| knee | 膝蓋 |
| label | 標籤 |
| laundry service | 洗衣服務 |
| lawn | 草坪 |

| | |
|---|---|
| leisure | 空閒；悠閒 |
| lipstick | 口紅；唇膏 |
| living room | 起居室 |
| lounge | 休息室 |
| luck | 運氣 |
| lunch | 午餐 |
| magazine | 雜誌 |
| male | 男性 |
| market | 市場 |
| medicine | 藥 |
| menu | 菜單 |
| message | 消息 |
| midnight | 午夜 |
| mile | 英里 |
| mop | 拖把 |
| mountain | 山脈 |
| music | 音樂 |
| nap | 小睡；打盹 |
| napkin | 餐巾；餐巾紙 |
| nationality | 國籍 |
| needle | 針 |

| | |
|---|---|
| newspaper | 報紙 |
| noise | 噪聲，雜音 |
| note | 筆記 |
| notice | 通知 |
| novel | 小說 |
| number | 數字 |
| officer | 官員；軍官 |
| oil-painting | 油畫 |
| one-way ticket | 單程票 |
| opera | 戲劇 |
| panda | 熊貓 |
| parking lot | 停車場 |
| partner | 搭檔；合作者 |
| passenger | 旅客 |
| passport | 護照 |
| peanut | 花生 |
| pearl | 珍珠 |
| perfume | 香水 |
| per night | 每晚 |
| pet | 寵物 |
| pill | 藥丸 |

| | |
|---|---|
| plane ticket | 飛機票 |
| price tag | 價簽 |
| room number | 房號 |
| room service | 客房送餐服務 |
| service charge | 服務費 |
| shopping center | 購物中心 |
| silk | 絲綢 |
| souvenir | 紀念品 |
| spoon | 匙；調羹 |
| staying guest | 住店客人 |
| style | 風格 |
| table cloth | 桌布 |
| toy | 玩具 |
| travel agency | 旅行社 |
| tray | 碟；盤子 |
| trouble | 麻煩 |
| vase | 花瓶 |
| VIP | 重要人物 |
| visa | 簽證 |
| wake-up call | 叫早服務 |

# Appendix II English Menu of Chinese Food

## 中餐英文菜譜

| | |
|---|---|
| 全體乳豬 | Roast whole suckling pig |
| 特色五福拼盤 | Special five varieties |
| 葡國碳燒肉 | Portuguese roast pork |
| 脆皮靚燒雞 | Crispy chicken |
| 湛江皇后水晶雞 | Zhanjiang Crystal chicken |
| 金牌回香雞 | Golden tasty chicken |
| 鹽香脆皮雞 | Salty crispy chicken |
| 高州蔥油雞 | Gaozhou style shallot flavor chicken |
| 蜜汁碳燒叉燒 | Honey charcoal pork |
| 碳燒靚排骨 | Charcoal spare ribs |
| 骨香乳鴿 | Tasty baby pigeon |
| 錦繡燒味拼盤 | Assorted barbecue meat |
| 新派鹵水拼盤 | New style soy sauce stewed meat |
| 新派鹵水掌翼 | New style soy sauce stewed goose wing and feet |
| 新派鹵水大腸頭 | New style soy sauce stewed pig's intestine |

| 新派鹵水肚仔 | New style soy sauce stewed pig's tomach |
| --- | --- |
| 新派鹵水腳仔 | New style soy sauce stewed pig's hoof |
| 鹽焗腎片 | Baked salty chicken kidney |
| 涼拌海蜇 | Marinated cold jelly fish |
| 刀拍黃瓜 | Marinated cold cucumber |
| 小食類 | Entrée |
| 日式海蜇 | Japanese style jelly fish |
| 日式八爪魚 | Japanese style octopus |
| 涼拌青瓜 | Marinated cold cucumber |
| 涼拌粉皮 | Marinated cold bean pasty |
| 蒜香腎片 | Garlic taste kidney |
| 蒜香豬耳仔 | Garlic taste pig's ear |
| 麻辣鳳爪 | Spicy hot chicken feet |
| 琥珀核桃 | Deep fried walnut in syrup |

# Appendix Ⅲ Chinese Snacks 中式小吃

中式早點

| 燒餅 | Clay oven rolls |
| --- | --- |
| 油條 | Fried bread stick |

| | |
|---|---|
| 韭菜盒 | Fried leek dumplings |
| 水餃 | Boiled dumplings |
| 蒸餃 | Steamed dumplings |
| 饅頭 | Steamed buns |
| 刈包 | Steamed sandwich |
| 飯糰 | Rice and vegetable roll |
| 蛋餅 | Egg cakes |
| 皮蛋 | century egg · thousand-year egg |
| 鹹鴨蛋 | Salted duck egg |
| 豆漿 | Soybean milk |

## 飯類

| | |
|---|---|
| 稀飯 | Rice porridge |
| 白飯 | Plain white rice |
| 油飯 | Glutinous oil rice |
| 糯米飯 | Glutinous rice |
| 滷肉飯 | Braised pork rice |
| 蛋炒飯 | Fried rice with egg |
| 地瓜粥 | Sweet potato congee |
| 麵類 | |
| 餛飩麵 | Wonton & noodles |

| | |
|---|---|
| 刀削麵 | Sliced noodles |
| 麻辣麵 | Spicy hot noodles |
| 麻醬麵 | Sesame paste noodles |
| 鴨肉麵 | Duck with noodles |
| 鱔魚麵 | Eel noodles |
| 烏龍麵 | Seafood noodles |
| 榨菜肉絲麵 | Pork · pickled mustard green noodles |
| 牡蠣細麵 | Oyster thin noodles |
| 板條 | Flat noodles |
| 米粉 | Rice noodles |
| 炒米粉 | Fried rice noodles |
| 冬粉 | Green bean noodles |
| 湯類 | |
| 魚丸湯 | Fish ball soup |
| 貢丸湯 | Meat ball soup |
| 蛋花湯 | Egg & vegetable soup |
| 蛤蜊湯 | Clams soup |
| 牡蠣湯 | Oyster soup |
| 紫菜湯 | Seaweed soup |
| 酸辣湯 | Sweet & sour soup |
| 餛飩湯 | Wonton soup |

| | |
|---|---|
| 豬腸湯 | Pork intestine soup |
| 肉羹湯 | Pork thick soup |
| 魷魚湯 | Squid soup |
| 花枝羹 | Squid thick soup |

# Appendix IV Chinese and Foreign Holidays 中外節日

國外主要節日

元旦（1月1日）——New Year's Day

成人節　（日本，1月的第二個星期一）——Coming-of-Age Day

情人節　（2月14日）——St.Valentine's Day (Valentine's Day)

狂歡節（巴西，二月中下旬）——Carnival

桃花節（日本女兒節，3月3日）——Peach Flower Festival (Doll's Festival)

國際婦女節（3月8日）——International Women's Day

聖帕特里克節（愛爾蘭，3月17日）——St.Patrick's Day

楓糖節（加拿大，3—4月）——Maple Sugar Festival

愚人節（4月1日）——Fool's Day

復活節（春分月圓後第一個星期日）——Easter

宋干節（泰國新年，4月13日）——Songkran Festival Day

食品節（新加坡，4月17日）──Food Festival

國際勞動節（5月1日）──International Labour Day

男孩節（日本，5月5日）──Boy's Day

母親節（5月的第二個星期日）──Mother's Day

把齋節（穆斯林一年一度的齋月）──Bamadan

開齋節（伊斯蘭教節日，4月或5月，回曆十月一日）──
Lesser Bairam

銀行休假日（英國，5月31日）──Bank Holiday

國際兒童節（6月1日）──International Children's Day

父親節（6月的第三個星期日）──Father's Day

仲夏節（北歐6月）──Mid-Summer Day

古爾邦節（伊斯蘭節，7月下旬）──Corban

筷子節（日本，8月4日）──Chopsticks Day

敬老節（日本，9月15日）──Old People's Day

啤酒節（德國十月節，10月10日）──Oktoberfest

南瓜節（北美10月31日）──Pumpkin Day

鬼節（萬聖節除夕，10月31日夜）──Halloween

萬聖節（11月1日）──All Saints' Day

感恩節（美國，11月最後一個星期四）──Thanksgiving

聖誕前夕（12月24日）──Christmas Eve

聖誕節（12月25日）──Christmas Day

節禮日（12月26日）──Boxing Day

新年除夕（12 月31日）——New Year's Eve (a bank holiday in many countries )

中國主要節日

春節（農曆一月一日）——Spring Festival (Chinese Lunar New Year)

元宵節（農曆一月十五日）——the Lantern Festival

植樹節（3月12日）——Arbor Day

清明節（4 月 5 日）——The Qingming (Pure Brightness) Festival; Tomb-Sweeping Festival

端午節（農曆五月初五）——the Dragon Boat Festival

中秋節（農曆八月十五）——Mid-Autumn (Moon) Festival

重陽節（農曆九月九日）——Double-Ninth Day

除夕（農曆十二月二十九日或三十日）——New Year's Eve

世界各國的國慶與獨立日

1月

1日 古巴解放日——Liberation Day (Cuba)

蘇丹獨立日——Independence Day (Sudan)

4日 緬甸獨立日——Independence Day (Myanmar/Burma)

18日 突尼西亞革命日——Revolution Day (Tunisia)

26日 澳大利亞日——Australia Day

印度共和國日──Repubic Day (India)

28日 盧安達民主日──Democracy Day (Rwanda)

2月

4日 斯里蘭卡國慶日──National Day (Srilanka)

5日 墨西哥憲法日──Constitution Day (Mexico)

6日 新西蘭國慶日──Waitangi Day (New Zealand)

7日 格林納達獨立日──Independence Day (Grenada)

11日 日本建國日──National Founding Day (Japan)

伊朗伊斯蘭革命勝利日──Anniversary of the Victory of the Islamic Revolution (Iran)

16日 美國華盛頓誕辰──Washington's Birthday (USA)

18日 甘比亞獨立日──Independence Day (Gambia)

23日 汶萊國慶日──National Day (Brunei Darussalam)圭亞那共和國日──Republic Day (Guiyana)

25日 科威特國慶日──National Day (Kuwait)

3月

3日 摩洛哥登基日──Enthronement Day (Morocco)

6日 加納獨立日──Independence Day (Ghana)

12日 模里西斯獨立日──Independence Day (Mauritius)

17日 愛爾蘭國慶日──National Day (Ireland)

23日 巴基斯坦日──Pakistan Day

25日 希臘國慶日──National Day (Greece)

26日 孟加拉獨立及國慶日——Independence & National Day (Bangladesh)

31日 馬耳他國慶日——National Day (Malta)

4月

4日 匈牙利國慶日——Liberation Day (Hungary)

塞內加爾獨立日——Independence Day (Senegal)

11日 烏干達解放日——Liberation Day (Uganda)

16日 丹麥女王日——Birthday of Her Majesty Queen Margrethe II (Denmark)

17日 敘利亞國慶日——National Day (Syria)

18日 辛巴威獨立日——Independence Day (Zimbabwe)

19日 委內瑞拉獨立節——Independence Day (Venezuela)

26日 獅子山共和國日——Republic Day (Sierra Leone)

坦尚尼亞聯合日——Union Day (Tanzania)

27日 多哥獨立日——Independence Day (Togo)

29日 日本天皇誕辰——Birthday of His Majesty the Emperor (Japan)

30日 荷蘭女王日——Official Celebration Day of the Birthday of Her Majesty Queen Beatrix (The Netherlands)

5月

9日 捷克與斯洛伐克國慶日——National Day (Czech & Slovakia)

17日 挪威憲法日——Constitution Day (Norway)

20日 喀麥隆國慶日——National Day (Cameroon)

25日 阿根廷5月革命紀念日——May 25‧1810 Revolution Day (Argentina)

約旦獨立日——Independence Day (Jordan)

6月

1日 突尼西亞勝利日——Victory Day (Tunisia)

西薩摩亞獨立日——Independence Day (Western Samoa)

2日 義大利共和國日——Foundation of Republic (Italy)

5日 丹麥憲法日——Constitution Day (Denmark)

塞席爾解放日——Liberation Day (Seychelles)

6日 瑞典國慶日——National Day (Sweden)

7日 乍得國慶日——National Day (Chad)

10日 葡萄牙國慶日——National/Portugal Day (Portugal)

12 日 菲律賓獨立日——Independence Day (The Philippines)

14日 英國女王官方生日——Official Birthday of Her Majesty Queen ElizabethⅡ (UK)

17日 冰島共和國日——Anniversary of the Proclamation of the Republic (Iceland)

23日 盧森堡國慶日——National Day (Luxembourg)

24日 西班牙國王陛下日——His Majesty the King's Day (Spain)

26日 馬達加斯加獨立日——Independence Day (Madagas

car)

27日 吉布地獨立日——Independence Day (Djibouti)

7月

1日 蒲隆地國慶日——National Day (Burundi)

加拿大日——Canada Day

盧安達獨立日——Independence Day (Rwanda)

4日 美國獨立日——Independence Day (USA)

5日 維德角獨立日——Independence Day (Cape Verde)

委內瑞拉獨立日——Independence Day (Venezuela)

6日 葛摩獨立日——Independence Day (Comoros)

11日 蒙古人民革命紀念日——Anniversary of the People's Revolution (Mongolia)

14日 法國國慶日——National/Bastille Day (France)

17日 伊拉克國慶日——National Day (Iraq)

20日 哥倫比亞國慶日——National Day (Union of Colombia)

21日 比利時國慶日——National Day (Belgium)

22日 波蘭國家復興節——Rebirth of Poland

23日 埃及國慶日——National Day (Egypt)

26日 利比亞獨立日——Independence Day (Liberia)

馬爾地夫獨立日——Independence Day (Maldives)

28日 秘魯獨立日——Independence Day (Peru)

30日 萬那杜獨立日——Independence Day (Vanuatu)

8月

1日 瑞士聯邦成立日——Foundation of the Confederation (Switzerland)

4日 布吉納法索國慶日——National Day (Burkina Faso)

5日 牙買加獨立日——Independence Day (Jamaica)

6日 玻利維亞獨立日——Independence Day (Bolivia)

10日 厄瓜多獨立日——Independence Day (Equador)

15日 剛果國慶日——National Day (The Gongo)

17日 加彭獨立日——Independence Day (Gabon)

19日 阿富汗獨立日——Independence Day (Afghanistan)

23日 羅馬尼亞國慶日——National Day (Romania)

31日 馬來西亞國慶日——National Day (Malaysia)

9月

1日 利比亞九月革命節——The Great 1stof September Revolution (Libya)

2日 越南國慶日——National Day (Vietnam)

3日 聖馬力諾國慶日——National Day (San Marino)

7日 巴西獨立日——Independence Day (Brazil)

9日 朝鮮共和國日——Day of the Founding of DPPK

12日 維德角國慶日——National Day (Cape Verde)

衣索匹亞人民革命日——The people's Revolution Day

(Ethiopia)

16日 墨西哥獨立節——Independence Day (Mexico)

18日 智利獨立日——Independence Day (Chile)

22 日 馬利宣布獨立日——Proclamation of Independence (Mali)

30日 波札那獨立日——Independence Day (Botswana)

10月

1日 賽普勒斯國慶日——National Day (Cyprus)

奈及利亞國慶日——National Day (Nigeria)

2日 幾內亞宣布獨立日——Proclamation of the Republic (Guinea)

9日 烏干達獨立日——Independence Day (Uganda)

10日 斐濟國慶日——National Day (Fiji)

12日 西班牙國慶日——National Day (Spain)

赤道幾內亞國慶節——National Day (Equatorial Guinea)

21日 索馬利亞十月革命節——21st October Revolution (Somalia)

24日 聯合國日——UN Day

尚比亞獨立日——Independence Day (Zambia)

26日 奧地利國慶日——National Day (Austria)

28日 希臘國慶節——National Day (Greece)

29日 土耳其共和國日——Proclamation of the Republic

(Turkey)

11月

1日 阿爾及利亞11月革命節——The Revolution Day of 1st November，1954 (Algeria)

11日 安哥拉獨立節——Independence Day (Angola)

15日 比利時國王日——King's Day (Belgium)

18日 阿曼國慶日——National Day (Oman)

19日 摩納哥國慶節——National Day (Monaco)

22日 黎巴嫩獨立日——Independence Day (Lebanon)

24日 薩伊第二共和國日——Anniversary of the Second Republic (Zaire)

28 日 茅利塔尼亞獨立日——Independence Day (Maritania)

29日 南斯拉夫共和國日——Republic Day (Yugoslavia)

12月

1日 中非國慶日——National Day (Central Africa)

2日 寮國國慶日——National Day (Laos)

阿 (拉伯)聯 (合)酋 (長國)國慶日——National Day (UAE，United Arab Emirates)

5日 泰國國王日——Birthday Anniversary of His Majesty King Bhumibol Adulyadej (Thailand)

6日 芬蘭獨立日——Independence Day (Finland)

7日 象牙海岸國慶日——National Day (Ivory Coast)

12日 肯亞獨立日——Independence Day (Kenya)

17日 不丹國慶節——National Day (Bhutan)

18日 尼日國慶日——National Day (Niger)

28日 尼泊爾國王生日——Birthday of His Majesty King Gyanendra (Nepal)

國家圖書館出版品預行編目(CIP)資料

飯店服務英語800句 / 趙志敏 主編. -- 第一版.
-- 臺北市：崧燁文化，2018.12

　　面；　　公分

ISBN 978-957-681-664-2(平裝)

1.英語 2.旅館業 3.會話

805.188　　　107021630

書　　名：飯店服務英語800句
作　　者：趙志敏 主編
發行人：黃振庭
出版者：崧燁文化事業有限公司
發行者：崧燁文化事業有限公司
E-mail：sonbookservice@gmail.com
粉絲頁　　　　　　網　址：
地　址：台北市中正區重慶南路一段六十一號八樓815室
8F.-815, No.61, Sec. 1, Chongqing S. Rd., Zhongzheng
Dist., Taipei City 100, Taiwan (R.O.C.)
電　話：(02)2370-3310 傳　真：(02) 2370-3210
總經銷：紅螞蟻圖書有限公司
地　址：台北市內湖區舊宗路二段121巷19號
電　話：02-2795-3656　傳真：02-2795-4100　網址：
印　刷 ：京峯彩色印刷有限公司（京峰數位）

定價：300 元
發行日期：2018 年 12 月第一版
◎ 本書以POD印製發行